He smiled, his eyes noting her wary stiffness

Kat knew the sudden tension in the room for what it was. Unwelcome, unexpected and undeniable.

Oh no, she wailed inwardly. Not Daniel Bishop. Not this worldly decadent capitalist who despised her as much as she ought to despise him. A man who didn't have a tender cherishing bone in his body—she couldn't be attracted to him! Surely she hadn't saved herself for him!

"What other tantalizing surprises have you prepared for me, and why?" he murmured. "I intend to know, Kathleen."

Kat found herself backing away. "Don't crowd me, Daniel—"

"The hell I will!" he said. "I'll do more than 'crowd.' You've had your fun tonight, Kathleen. Now it's my turn...."

SUSAN NAPIER was born on Valentine's Day, so perhaps it is only fitting that she should become a romance writer. She started out as a reporter for New Zealand's largest evening newspaper before resigning to marry the paper's chief reporter. After the birth of their two children she did some freelancing for a film production company and then settled down to write her first romance. "Now," she says, "I am in the enviable position of being able to build my career around my home and family."

Books by Susan Napier

HARLEQUIN PRESENTS

HARLEQUIN ROMANCE

Don't miss any of our special offers. Write to us at the following address for information on our newest releases.

Harlequin Reader Service
901 Fuhrmann Blvd., P.O. Box 1397, Buffalo, NY 14240
Canadian address: P.O. Box 603,
Fort Erie, Ont. L2A 5X3

SUSAN NAPIER

the love conspiracy

Harlequin Books

TORONTO • NEW YORK • LONDON
AMSTERDAM • PARIS • SYDNEY • HAMBURG
STOCKHOLM • ATHENS • TOKYO • MILAN

For my sons,
Simon and Benjamin

Harlequin Presents first edition March 1990
ISBN 0-373-11252-1

Original hardcover edition published in 1989
by Mills & Boon Limited

CHAPTER ONE

'A STRIPPER, Daniel! She's a *stripper*!' Adelaide Bishop's voice quivered with outrage.

'Actress, Mother, not stripper,' her son corrected her absently, calmly dividing his attention between his scrambled eggs and the financial section of the morning newspaper which was neatly folded beside his plate.

'An actress who *plays* a stripper—as far as I can see, there isn't any difference,' Adelaide replied, irritated by his lack of reaction to the shocking news just imparted by the other, now absent, occupant of the breakfast table. 'She still takes her clothes off in public . . . you can hardly call that kind of performance a *play*. No wonder it ended up in some awful little studio theatre; a *legitimate* director would never touch such trash.' Her thin haughty face, remarkably smooth for a woman in her sixties, tightened further as her son failed to instantly agree. 'Daniel, are you listening to me?'

'Of course I am.' Daniel gave his mother a smile of practised patience. The blandness of the smile made the dark, symmetrical face almost too handsome, but it was saved from characterlessness by the mystery of the surprisingly light blue eyes beneath the thick, dark brows, and by the two wings of ice-grey that streaked the midnight hair at his temples. They lay like devils' horns shimmering in the darkness, a warning to those tempted to trust the charming smile that here was a man not necessarily on the side of the angels.

'Well, you don't sound very concerned. Do you *want* your only nephew to marry a woman who takes her clothes off for money?'

It was on the tip of Daniel's cynical tongue to observe that wasn't that, in essence, what marriage was all about—the purchase of a woman's 'favours' in exchange for financial

7

security? Particularly in the circles in which he moved. But in deference to domestic peace he said merely, 'Of course not. But I think you're worrying prematurely about this girl——'

'Prematurely? He's asked her to *marry* him, Daniel, before he has even introduced her! And she's hardly a girl—she's nearly three years older than Todd, and probably decades older in experience. Of course, it was *her* idea to keep the relationship secret, Todd would never be so devious . . . he's so infatuated he'd be putty in her hands! And why spring this all on us *now*? Why invite her to stay *this* weekend? I'll tell you why, Daniel: it's a blatant attempt to blackmail us into appearing to sanction this . . . this impossible *liaison*. If she appears at your engagement party as a house-guest, naturally people are going to assume that she's socially acceptable. There are going to be some extremely important and influential friends here tomorrow night; what am I going to say when they ask about her? That's Cat, the stripper, my grandson's fiancée? Can you imagine the humiliation? And goodness knows what dirt the Press will dig up about her if it becomes common knowledge. You heard what he said, he doesn't know what her background is and doesn't care! Even her *name* reveals her lack of breeding. What kind of woman calls herself after an animal? And Todd expects me to welcome the prospect of this vulgar woman sharing my *home*!'

'I'm sure he realises it's not going to be that simple,' said Daniel drily, discreetly checking the flat gold watch which hung on a fine-link gold chain from the waistcoat of his navy pin-striped suit, his mind already reaching ahead to his meticulously planned day. 'He's gone to tell Sharon, hasn't he? Perhaps motherly dismay might carry more weight with him at the moment than anything we can say.'

'Oh, Sharon . . .' Adelaide dismissed her daughter-in-law with a wave of her beringed left hand. 'Sharon has no influence over the boy, she's always been far too soft on him for his own good. She'll probably tell him she's looking forward to meeting his little tramp. But *naturally* she'll back up any action we take.'

Naturally. It was a brave woman, or man, who openly opposed Adelaide's expressed wishes or incontrovertible opinions, which made it hard for Daniel to believe that Todd seriously intended to marry someone totally unacceptable to the family. Todd had inherited some of his mother's gentleness as well as his father's financial acumen, and he preferred co-existence to confrontation. No wonder Adelaide blamed the girl for the situation that had arisen, though whether she had deliberately set out to ensnare a rich husband was open to question. He folded his paper and stood. 'Well, whatever you decide to do, Mother, I'm sure you'll handle it beautifully. You always do.' Daniel stooped to kiss the porcelain brow under the artfully arranged silver hair, confident he could leave the domestic details to a practised schemer. This wouldn't be the first time that Adelaide had faced a challenge to family unity from a rank outsider.

'I have a late meeting this afternoon, by the way,' he told her as he picked up the black leather briefcase beside his chair and strode towards the open french doors through which dappled morning sunlight warmed the small, elegant breakfast-room. 'So don't expect me home before seven-thirty.'

'But you *will* be here for dinner, Daniel,' his mother ordered imperiously. 'I want this woman to be quite sure that she doesn't belong here. I want her to realise that under no circumstances will we be blackmailed into accepting her as a Bishop!'

Daniel slid into the back seat of the grey Mercedes with a smiling nod at the man holding the door. He felt a certain amount of detached sympathy for Todd's social-climbing actress. Whether she was a cunning, ambitious, hard-eyed bitch, or genuinely 'in love' with the man of her dreams, she would be no match for Adelaide. The weapons of polite society were different from those of the street, but no less effective in despatching a victim. Adelaide Bishop was such a skilled practitioner of razor-sharp manners and humiliating snubs that even the wealthy, self-confident inhabitants of her own social circle feared to displease her.

Daniel sighed as he retrieved a sheaf of papers from the combination-lock briefcase and spread them out on his lap. Dinner would prove to be boringly unpleasant, but he knew that, as head of the family, he could not escape the duty. He would be required to exert his own particular brand of brutally civilised intimidation. Ten years of striding the inner corridors of New Zealand's financial establishment had honed Daniel's talent for cloaking his ruthlessness beneath a bland, fastidious charm that lulled opponents into a false sense of security until the very moment the trap closed around them. Rex, Bishop was now the country's leading merchant bank, thanks to Daniel's driving ambition and skill at playing power games, and the Bishop family fortune was healthier than it had ever been before. In the unlikely event that Todd's girlfriend dug her heels in over making a discreet exit from her rich lover's life, there was always money. Daniel had yet to meet a woman whose price he couldn't judge at first glance—and pay, if he felt so inclined. At worst, this one would merely be an expensive nuisance; at best, a silly girl who had got out of her depth. Either way, it wasn't something he needed dwell on.

'Mmm . . .' Kathleen Kendon stretched luxuriously as she climbed out of the Lotus Esprit and leant her long body against the engine-warmed bonnet to take a good look at the house before her. Not so much a house as a mansion, she thought, her wide mouth curving into a generous smile of anticipation. Three storeys of white colonial perfection set in an acre of manicured grounds—curving crew-cut lawns, neatly patterned flowerbeds and a thick screen of trees and shrubs lining the high brick walls which hid the house from the curious eyes of the passer-by and the incurious eyes of equally rich, exclusive, privacy-conscious neighbours. The red gravel drive that the Lotus had carelessly scattered was raked in soothing lines to the foot of the wide marble stairway which led through tall, white, fluted columns to the heavy panelled door with its solid brass fittings. Neat triple rows of sashed windows with elegant dark blue shutters marched away on either side of the covered entranceway, attesting to the fact that the interior of the house was probably as rigidly symmetrical as the exterior. A beautiful, serene façade that made Kat wonder whether the inhabitants were similarly serene.

'Like it?' Todd Bishop crunched around to join her, carrying Kat's slightly battered overnight case in one hand and the jacket of his grey three-piece suit in the other.

Kat tilted her head teasingly. 'Well . . . it doesn't have the unique ambience of thirty-eight, Stanton Street, but I suppose it'll do, just for the weekend.'

Todd laughed. The house that Kat shared with four friends was in a very seedy part of the inner city as yet undiscovered by concrete-and-glass developers. It was wooden and white, but there any resemblance to Todd's home ended abruptly. The landlord, who owned several of the houses in the street, all distinctly askew with age, refused to waste money upgrading premises that he hoped to one day sacrifice to the wreckers' ball at enormous profit for himself. However, seedy as it was, the friendships forged and sustained within the walls of number thirty-eight made it more nearly a home to Kat than any other she had known in her twenty-three years.

'Do we go in now?' she asked, as Todd made no move to lead the way. 'Or were you intending to pitch a tent for me on the lawn and ruin all this lovely symmetry?'

Todd's smile faded and he looked a trifle uncomfortable. Kat hid a smile. If Todd was regretting the invitation, it was just too bad, she wasn't leaving now. She had been looking forward to this weekend of luxury for a fortnight—her first glimpse of how the other half lived.

'Er . . . Kat, there's something——'

'We're being watched.'

'What?' Todd jerked around, his broad young shoulders relaxing as he saw the man standing in the open doorway atop the flight of stairs. 'Oh, that's Seth.'

'Your butler? He doesn't look like a butler,' Kat commented as she took the initiative and began taking long, easy strides across the gravel. True, the man at the top of the stairs was wearing a traditional suit, but he was short and very muscular with a thick neck, grizzled grey hair and small, hard grey eyes that watched with uncomfortable shrewdness the two approaching.

'Well, he's not really a butler as such, he's a bit more than that,' said Todd, hurrying to catch up with her. 'But look, Kat, hang on a minute. I have to tell you something——'

Kat paused and smiled kindly at the slightly worried expression on the handsome face that tagged behind. 'Don't worry, Todd, I won't disgrace you.' She guessed the reason for his nervousness. 'I do know how to behave in polite society, you know.'

It hadn't escaped her notice that in the couple of months they had been seeing each other Todd had been careful never to take her anywhere they might be seen by his family or his own circle of friends. Kat had been amused rather than offended, because she sensed that Todd's reasons for the secrecy had been protective of her, rather than arrant snobbery. It had taken him this long to realise that she was a very self-possessed young woman, capable of holding her own in any company, however exalted.

In fact, she had no doubt that it was because the two of them were so very different that Todd was attracted in the first place. She was totally unlike the deb type of female who apparently made up his usual social circle. The previous year Todd had graduated from university with an honours degree in business and economics, and now he had his feet firmly placed on the career ladder that would eventually lead him to a directorship of the family bank. He was a young man who had impressed Kat as knowing exactly where he was going and why. The fact that he seemed to want to take Kat with him was as flattering as it was puzzling. Todd, nice as he was, was a genuine, dyed-in-the-wool conservative at heart. A woman like Kat would be a handicap to that carefully planned career, not an asset, and Todd didn't appear to be a man of impulse, despite his youthful appreciation of fun.

On one level, however, Kat wasn't at all surprised by the

persistence of his pursuit. Ever since the age of fourteen, when she had blossomed abruptly to her full height and stature, Kat had been on the receiving end of male attentions of one kind or the other . . . usually the other. But it wasn't only the tawny red-gold hair, tawny eyes and tawny skin that had earned her her nickname. She also possessed a feline love of creature comforts, combined with a very definitely cat-like independence of thought and spirit that frustrated many a suitor, misled into thinking that her lazy air of sensuality was an open invitation to all-comers.

'Of course you do, Kat,' Todd hastened to assure her as they resumed climbing, 'but you——'

'And if I get stuck, I can always fake it, can't I?' Kat tossed him a sideways grin that elicited a weak smile in return. Kat was a first-class mimic. Ten minutes of observation and she could slip into anyone's skin. She had got herself out of many a sticky situation in her eventful life by subtly flattering someone with a reflection of their own personality, or dragging out a suitable one from her rag-bag of memories. It was part of the reason for her immense self-possession.

'Kat——' The faintest trace of a whine in Todd's normally deep voice was cut off by the bit-more-than-a-butler.

'Mr Todd. Mrs Bishop expected you some time ago . . . for afternoon tea.'

'Yes, I know, we were held up,' Todd told him with a nervous grin, handing over Kat's suitcase to a rather battered hand. The hand of a fighter, thought Kat, as she noticed the flattened knuckles.

'He means I held him up,' Kat said. 'I'm afraid that my internal clock runs permanently slow, particularly on Fridays.'

'Er . . . Seth, this is Kat Kendon. My . . . guest for the weekend.'

'Miss Kendon.' The grey eyes gave nothing away as they looked at the lovely young woman smiling at him out of sleepy golden eyes. Unbelievable as it seemed, given what little he had been told about Todd's unexpected fiancée, she wasn't wearing an ounce of make-up, not even lipstick on that wide, full mouth. And yet still she looked gorgeous . . . and tall, several inches taller than her companion in her flat sandals.

'Six feet in stockings,' Kat murmured gravely as she followed the direction of his gaze, and thought she detected the twinge of a smile on the hard line of Seth's mouth.

'Your grandmother is still in the drawing-room, Mr Todd. I'll take Miss Kendon's bag up to the Pink Room.'

'Thanks. Come on, Kat, we'd better see her before she goes up to change for dinner.' Todd pulled Kat out of the early evening sunlight into the cool interior of the house. While Seth mounted the long curve of marble staircase to their right, Kat was led across a white-tiled foyer, relieved only by flourishes of flowers in large antique urns and a jewel-bright rug on the floor which looked so worn that it had to be genuine antique Persian. As they passed into the wide hallway, Kat caught a glimpse of a huge oil painting hanging on the long white wall of the first marble landing. It was an abstract, totally incomprehensible from a brief view, and very cool with its combination of blues, greens and greys.

Todd's hand was on the ornate brass handle of the double-panelled door at the end of the hallway when he halted their rapid progress.

'Kat . . . if you . . . you won't let me down, will you?'

'Of course I won't,' said Kat, puzzled by his vehemence. 'But——'

'There isn't time to tell you now. I should have before, but . . . well . . . please, Kat, just go along with everything.'

'OK . . .' Kat would have said more, but Todd had already opened the door. They went into a long, high-ceilinged rectangular room which was made to seem even larger by the pale cream carpet and painted walls. The cool frigidity of the décor was softened and accented by the richness of dark wood furnishings and the deep, vibrating colours of the embroidered upholstery and heavily framed paintings which lined the walls. At the far end of the room, french doors, framed by cream damask silk curtains, opened out on to pale paving stones surrounding a huge rectangular pool, an aching glitter of blue, reflecting the profusion of heavily flowered shrubs and trees which enclosed its Mediterranean splendour. Just in front of the doors, preserving the exquisite decorative balance of the room, were two women, seated on a crimson and cream striped settee. They had been talking in muted tones as Todd and Kat entered, but now a heavy silence fell.

Oh, dear. Kat felt the mischievous urge to genuflect as they approached the upright, silver-haired figure who was attired, even in the oppressive heat of an Auckland summer's day, in a pale blue silk suit with matching blouse. Not the casually rumpled silk favoured by modern fashion, but the classic stiff, heavy kind, expensively embossed with a paler hue. Thin as a rail and elegant to the tips of her manicured fingernails, thought Kat with a sigh, suddenly feeling acutely underdressed in her simple cotton sunfrock. But at least she was comfortable. In spite of her cool air, Todd's grandmother had to be sweltering under all that elegance. The finely moulded face, beautifully made-up, looked as stiff as the silk of her suit, and the frosted blue eyes indicated that the woman was not in a mood to be easily impressed. The other woman, less slim and with tobacco-brown hair and Todd's hazel eyes, looked more approachable but no less constrained by the dignified atmosphere of the room.

'I'm sorry we didn't make it for tea,' Todd said with apologetic lightness, 'but Kat wasn't quite ready when I arrived to pick her up. Grandmother, may I present Kat Kendon. Kat, this is my grandmother, Adelaide Bishop, and my mother, Sharon Bishop.'

Kat smiled and murmured a greeting, thinking: now why on earth did he say that? Why be politely evasive with Seth, but ditch her in the soup with his family?

'Miss Kendon.' Adelaide Bishop's regal head dipped, giving her eyes time to travel slowly from the red-gold waves tumbling untidily around bare feminine shoulders, down over the lushly ripe curves revealed by the sundress Todd had told her was 'just right' to wear to his home, down the long, long journey to her casual footwear. If Kat felt underdressed before, now she felt positively naked . . . but I should be used to it by now, she thought with an inner grin. She continued to smile patiently, willing to put up with a matriarchal once-over for the sake of a few days' masquerade as one of the idle rich.

'Kat, Grandmother, everyone calls her Kat,' Todd corrected cheerfully, with less than his usual tact. It was obvious from Adelaide Bishop's pained expression that she had never used a nickname in her life.

'Actually, my name is Kathleen,' Kat said soothingly.

'You're Irish?'

'I'm not sure,' said Kat, with such innocent honesty that there was a moment's shocked silence. Kat smiled at Sharon Todd and surprised a fugitive smile which vanished as she tried to flush it out with some direct attention. 'I'm so pleased to meet you both, Todd has told me so much about you.' Which was a polite fiction. Todd had been rather vague about his family, other than to say that his grandmother was extremely domineering, his mother rather vague and his uncle—the one whose engagement they were celebrating this weekend—a workaholic fixated by the concept of family duty.

'And Todd has told us much about you,' said Adelaide Bishop with equal politeness, smoothly recovering from that startling conversational foray. 'Do sit down, Miss Kendon. It's a little late to offer you tea, and too early for drinks, but perhaps you can tell us something about yourself before you go up to bathe and change for dinner.'

Kat sat down in an antique, satin-backed chair that proved to be as comfortable as it was old and beautiful, amused at the variety of interpretations that could be read into the polite invitation. If she had been the over-sensitive type, she might consider herself just chastised for lateness, informed that her clothing was unsuitable and that her cleanliness was suspect!

'I understand that you're an actress, Miss Kendon?' Adelaide Bishop enquired after a heavy pause.

'Kat,' interrupted Todd quite unnecessarily. 'She likes to

be called Kat.'

His grandmother's mouth tucked in tightly, showing the age lines that were carefully masked with cosmetics when her face was in smooth repose. She must have been an extremely beautiful woman once, thought Kat, and was growing old only with extreme reluctance, fighting every inch of the way with every expensive weapon in a cosmetician's arsenal.

'Please, call me Kathleen,' Kat said gently, unwilling to force the woman to compromise her dignity. She frowned admonishingly at Todd hovering beside her. He merely shrugged smilingly in reply.

'Kathleen.' The haughty vowels turned it into a stranger's name. 'Todd tells us that you're on the stage, an *actress*.'

The faintly strained emphasis spoke volumes. Todd must have told her about Kat's one-woman show. Kat wasn't ashamed of it, but she did think that Todd might have been a bit more circumspect, given his grandmother's obviously old-fashioned morals.

'Well, no, I'm not really an actress,' she began, endeavouring to explain that it was her talent for mimicry, not acting, that had led to her intermittent career on the stage. 'People label me an actress, and I model sometimes, too, but both are just euphemisms for what I *really* do.'

As soon as the words were out of her mouth Kat paused, realising the unfortunate connotations that could and were being applied, judging from the congealing expression on Adelaide's rigid face. Her blue eyes were even chillier than ever. Oh, dear, how do you politely inform a correct old lady that you're not the prostitute that you just hinted you were, without sounding either outrageously tacky or suspiciously defensive? Mentally floundering at the prospect of the task, Kat cast a pleading look at Todd, and to her disconcertment surprised an expression of smugness rather than amusement or embarrassment on his face. Hey, what was going on here?

The moment to redeem herself was lost. In the ensuing onslaught of questions about her background, Kat found herself even more at sea. This wasn't so much a conversation

as an interrogation! And Todd was just standing there,
letting her fend for herself without any support whatsoever.
He wouldn't even meet her questioning gaze. Between them
his grandmother and his mother laid bare the raw,
unvarnished details of her life: the loss of her parents, about
whom she knew so little, in an accident when she was three;
her total lack of relatives; her upbringing as a State ward in a
small orphanage; the fact that she had never held a job for
more than a year since she had left school, and the
orphanage, at sixteen.

As the excruciating minutes inched by, Kat, usually highly
tolerant of humanity's infinite variety, began to secretly
simmer. It *wasn't* just over-sensitivity. Adelaide Bishop was
being offensive. Oh, it was all very discreet and very polite,
but Kat was definitely being got at. And there was nothing
she could do about it without resorting to an open rudeness
that would give the determined old lady even more
ammunition in her covert campaign to expose the appalling
gaps in Kat's social and intellectual education. There were
few people Kat had met whom she didn't like, and even
fewer who didn't like her. Adelaide Bishop qualified on both
counts. But why? And why did Kat get the feeling that,
although Sharon Bishop asked questions which were every
bit as pointed as her mother-in-law's, her heart wasn't really
in it?

If Kat had been less secure she would have wilted, but in
spite of her lazy air she possessed a core of steel. She knew
that the only respect that really mattered was the respect one
accorded oneself . . . the rest of the world was measured
against that yardstick. However, her pride was definitely
pricked, all the more because she had the very distinct feeling
that she had been deliberately set up for all this hostility.

At last, with the satisfied smile of one who feels she has
achieved a valuable victory, Adelaide Bishop rose and
suggested regally that perhaps it was time to prepare for
dinner.

'We do enjoy a certain formality in dining in this house,

Miss Kendon, but please don't be embarrassed if you have nothing quite suitable. We shall understand.'

The condescension rankled, considering that they all knew that Kat had been invited for a weekend which included a formal ball. 'Oh, I brought plenty to wear,' Kat lied with a dazzling smile. 'I know that burnt orange clashes horribly with my hair, but I *do* so love vivid colours . . . and at least I can be sure of standing out in a crowd!'

Adelaide Bishop's pale complexion was milked of a little of its colour, and for the first time she brought her attack out in the open. 'I hope you understand, Miss Kendon, that this celebration has been planned for some time and that it is for Daniel and Clarissa *only*. There will be no announcement from you and Todd, either publicly or privately, tomorrow evening. You are merely a guest in this house and will behave accordingly. As far as this family is concerned, there *is* no engagement. I can only be thankful that Todd has had the decency not to flaunt his contempt for his mother and me by giving you a ring. You might ponder that, Miss Kendon, and wonder whether perhaps your complacency is a trifle hasty.'

She withdrew while Kat's mouth was still hanging open, Todd's mother quickly followed suit after a nervous smile at her son. Kat's teeth snapped shut with an audible click as all was suddenly explained. She spun around, golden eyes molten with temper.

'Now, Kat, you must admit I did try to warn you——' Todd backed away from her intimidating height, holding up his hands, half laughing, half serious.

'Not very hard,' said Kat grimly. 'May I ask, as if I didn't already know, where that old harridan got the idea that you and I were engaged?'

Todd choked at the description of a woman who considered herself the epitome of a lady. 'I'm sorry, Kat, truly I am, but I wouldn't have done it if I wasn't sure that you could stand up to her. You're the only woman I know who could.'

Kat's eyes narrowed as her suspicions were confirmed. 'I

don't know whether that's flattery or an insult. And if I'm
fighting your battles for you, young Todd, don't I at least
have the right to know *why*?'

'Yes, you do,' he said soberly. 'I'm sorry, Kat, but I
thought that if I told you beforehand you might not agree to
help me . . .' He spread his hands with a charmingly boyish
gesture of helplessness, and watched Kat's fierce expression
soften. Lovely Kat, so hard in some ways, yet so impossibly
naïve in others. She was a sucker for a sob story and he ought
to feel guily, but he didn't. She was needed more than she
could know.

'Come upstairs. I'll show you your room and we can talk.
Now that you've seen Grandmother in action, I'm sure you'll
understand, whereas you probably wouldn't have before. It's
not purely selfish, you see . . . there's someone else involved.
And when I tell you, well . . . you'll see that you're the only
person I can trust to help me . . .'

CHAPTER TWO

KAT frowned at herself in the mirror. Something wasn't right with the red dress. Was it the gold shoes and belt? The knee-skimming length? Or the dramatically plunging wrapover neckline, which had always looked so discreet on the dress's slim owner?

She turned away with a sigh. Who was she to judge? The fact that she could look gorgeous in a sack—scruffy, but gorgeous—had ruined what clothes-sense she might have been born with. She relied on her friends' advice whenever she went shopping, and consequently her wardrobe was a jumbled hotchpotch of differing tastes, none of which seemed to co-ordinate.

Kat's only saving grace was her scarves. Kat could do things with a strip of hand-dyed silk that made strong men go weak at the knees and women weep with envy. She wore one now, drifting from her belt, a vivid shade of green that should have clashed horribly, but didn't. It was the only thing she *was* sure of.

It was also the only thing that wasn't borrowed. Everything else—except her underwear, of course—was courtesy of her house-mates. The dress was Colleen's—a talented but still aspiring actress with a flair for the dramatic which Kat admired; the shoes were Freya's—a theatre wardrobe mistress who bemoaned the fact that although she was nearly a foot shorter than Kat her feet were of a size; and the belt was Allan's. He was a leatherworker who belonged to the same craft co-operative as the other male member of the household, Jeff, a jewellery designer. It was Jeff's gold watch that she was wearing, and which he had cunningly—without her knowledge—set twenty minutes fast in order to mitigate the infuriating

21

effects of her normally chronic lateness.

Kat sorted vaguely through the barely used tubes and compacts she had tipped untidily out on the richly polished surface of the rosewood dressing-table. Make-up was something else she often didn't bother with unless she was working, but in a way tonight *was* work. She really ought to be furious at Todd for his deception, for the way he had presumed on their brief friendship, but she was too kind-hearted to walk out on him when he was so obviously desperate.

For Todd was wretchedly in love: with someone Horribly Unsuitable, someone he didn't dare present to his family for fear that they would crush her fragile spirit. Todd went on at some length about his lady-love, a sweet-natured, innocent, gentle, highly sensitive creature of nineteen who was studying violin at Auckland University's Music School. Her family had no social cachet, let alone money, and Anna was dedicated but modest about her talent as a violinist, so there was no hope of a socially redeeming career as a brilliant soloist.

Kat briefly harboured the unkind thought that darling Anna sounded a little bit drippy, but there was no doubt that Todd had it badly. The usually jaunty, self-confident young man paced up and down the pink and gold guest bedroom, looking anguished.

His grandmother would make a meal of Anna and still be hungry! Anna wasn't equipped to deal with the withering hostility that Adelaide Bishop would aim her way, Anna didn't have enough self-confidence . . . she already harboured the silly notion that Todd was too good for her; rejection from his family would devastate her. She would refuse to marry him if she thought that it would mean his alienation from the home and family that meant so much to him. Family was very important to Anna. Todd had been trying to protect her from the inevitable for some time, but she was beginning to ask about his family. He *had* to come up with a way of insinuating her into the Bishops' good graces with a minimum of damaging unpleasantness.

Then he met Kat. Strong, independent, self-confident Kat, champion of the underdog, squelcher of snobs and hypocrites. She had treated him with encouragingly sisterly casualness . . . and she was the only woman he had ever met whom he could imagine standing up to his grandmother. Kat was his godsend.

'I'm also a penniless, jumped-up little actress from nowhere,' Kat supplied drily, way ahead of him, 'a social-climbing gold-digger expressly designed to strike terror into the hearts of the aristocracy. And when you buckle under and finally give this scarlet tramp the elbow, your family will be so relieved that they'll positively *beam* at the production of a nice, quiet, well-behaved, malleable little middle-class musician.'

'Something like that,' Todd admitted humbly.

'*Exactly* like that.' Kat had given him an earful about respect and trust, and his shabby treatment of her pride, and he had been meekly penitent. Both of them had known that the end result would be her capitulation. Helping a pair of star-crossed lovers while simultaneously hoisting Adelaide Bishop with her own snobbish petard was an irresistible prospect to an incurably practical romantic like Kat. The plan was daring, and quite uncharacteristic of Todd's prosaic mind. It also had loopholes in it that Kat could drive a bus through but, as Todd pointed out, he didn't really have anything to lose. Neither did Kat. In fact, it could be fun to act such an outrageous part.

'Just for the weekend, Kat.' Todd was quick to pick up her glimmer of mischievous enthusiasm. 'I can take care of Mother . . . she won't openly support either side in any case, not until there's a clear winner. But Daniel will. Emotionally he's a very fastidious person. He usually leaves unpleasant domestic details, like choosing the family brides, to Grandmother, but if he thinks my behaviour might compromise the reputation of the family or bank he'll definitely put his foot down.'

'Are you saying that he let your grandmother arrange *his* engagement?' asked Kat incredulously.

Todd shrugged. 'It's a kind of recent family tradition—that's why I'm in such a panic about Anna. Grandmother linked up my own parents and my aunt Diana and *her* husband. Once she has Daniel and Clarissa safely hitched, she'll be lining *me* up in her sights. Daniel's thirty-six. I don't think he's all that keen on marriage, but I suppose he feels it's time he did his duty and produced some heirs. Most of his time and energy is taken up at the bank, you see, and he's pretty cyncial about women in general, so he just let Grandmother trot out some suitable candidates and picked one. We've known Clarissa's family for years . . . her father is heir to some minor British title or other, and they have pots of money. A perfect genetic mix in Grandmother's view.'

'I think it's obscene,' said Kat firmly. 'I thought *you* were conservative, but your uncle must be positively archaic! What a pity that genetic research hasn't perfected cloning He could reproduce without any of that tacky, emotional, hands-on stuff.'

'I suppose Daniel would *seem* fairly conservative, especially to someone like you,' Todd selected his words cautiously, probably trying hard to present his uncle in a loyal light, 'but it's difficult for him to be otherwise. I mean, reputation is pretty important in financial circles. One newspaper article called him one of New Zealand's "financial priesthood",' a lopsided grin, 'and as such I guess he has to be above reproach. You might find him pretty cool and reserved, but he's always like that with people he doesn't know . . . he actually has beautiful manners and a terrifically impeccable taste in clothes . . .'

Kat was left with a decidedly woolly picture of a man damned with faint praise. It sounded as if Daniel Bishop would be easy to shock. Rather like a potato, in fact . . . very starchy and bland beneath his *impeccable* jacket, and very boring as a constant diet. Maybe, she speculated wildly, there was even a whiff of latent homosexuality in his apparent indifference to women.

Kat was both surprised and pleased to find herself ready when Todd came back to collect her for dinner, even though he was only fifteen minutes late . . . her usual runover was twenty.

'What, no white tie and tails?' she laughed as she flung open the door and saw his light grey suit. She tucked her arm in his as she drew him out of the elegantly furnished bedroom and into the hall. 'And no dinner gong, either. What kind of cheap joint is this?'

'There are chiming clocks in all the rooms.' Todd grinned as they strolled down the hallway, stopping now and then so that Kat could look at the paintings lining the white walls. 'Daniel collects investment art and antique clocks. It's his only interest outside the bank. And opera, of course. He and Clarissa are patrons.'

'Of course,' said Kat drily. She had never been to an opera in her life, and believed that art was something you judged with your heart and not your wallet. As for clocks, they were the bane of her existence, and she had refused to even notice the one in her bedroom.

'Which is your room?' she asked curiously as they progressed past a series of white-panelled doors.

Todd's eyes twinkled. 'Opposite wing, I'm afraid. Grandmother has made sure that you're well out of temptation's path.'

'Sort of like an isolation ward,' said Kat, not at all insulted. She rather liked the idea of lonely splendour; she certainly didn't get any of that in the cramped quarters of thirty-eight, Stanton Street. 'Is this a guest wing, or something?'

'Mostly. Except for Daniel. He has the double suite next to your room. Most likely he'll have instructions to keep an ear out for creaking floorboards in the night,' said Todd, a strange look of smugness on his face.

'I'll be sure to do some solitary lurking,' said Kat. She remembered the door on the other side of the gratifyingly modern bathroom. It had been locked, but there had been no key. She envisaged herself blundering in on a de-jacketed potato in the bath and giggled. 'I hope we don't have to share facilities.'

'Don't worry, Daniel is pretty self-contained,' said Todd, adding wryly, 'In more ways than one. He has a penthouse apartment in the bank building, but he doesn't spend much time there. Grandmother likes to keep the family together here.'

'Why don't *you* break out and get a place of your own? Or borrow his? Then you could see Anna whenever you liked, without having to run the gauntlet of everyone's opinion.'

'Because this is mine. It's my home,' said Todd with a simplicity that Kat envied. Home, for her, had always been within herself. 'In spite of all the disadvantages of living here, it's my home and I'm proud of it. Four generations of Bishop sons have lived here with their families. It's our heritage. It will be my sons' heritage, and Daniel's. Whatever our disagreements, the bottom line is that the Bishops stick together. That's why I want Grandmother's blessing for Anna. Because once Anna has that, she'll be one of us. A Bishop. Grandmother will be fighting *for* her, not against her.'

As long as she toes Grandmother's line, thought Kat. Poor Anna . . . and Todd was deliberately keeping her in the dark about what she was marrying into. Ah, well, it wasn't Kat's problem, what happened *after* . . . 'Sounds a bit Mafia-ish to me. Family honour and all that.'

'Speaking of which.' Todd stopped at the bottom of the staircase, searching in his pocket. 'Will you do me the honour of wearing these?'

He looked slightly embarrassed, and the reason was obvious. The glittering ruby and diamond choker and large matching engagement ring were in questionable taste. Kat didn't have to ask whether they were real . . . the sparkle was blinding.

'Thank you,' said Kat drily. 'That should add just the

right mercenary touch.' She let Todd clasp the heavy choker around her bare throat, removing the fine gold chain she always wore and putting it in her bra for safe-keeping. 'Uh-uh.' She put her hand behind her back when he tried to put the ring on her finger. 'Let's just leave it threateningly "unofficial", shall we? Call it silly ethics on my part . . . or superstition.' Her wide, direct eyes rose to his. 'And if you were thinking of insulting our newly honest friendship by telling me I could keep one or other of these afterwards . . . don't.' It was gently said, but the warning in her voice made Todd meekly replace the ring-box in his pocket.

They crossed the echoing entrance hall, heading for what Kat guessed was a formal dining-room. As they stepped on to the muffled softness of the Persian rug, they heard Adelaide Bishop's clear, carrying voice float out of the half-open door.

'. . . absolutely appalling *giant* of a girl, Daniel, I was almost afraid for the furniture, and no breeding at all. She doesn't even have the saving grace of an *education*, and completely brazen about her ignorance. I can't imagine *what* Todd finds so fascinating . . .'

'You must admit, Adelaide, that she is beautiful,' came Sharon Bishop's gentle interruption of the blanket condemnation, and Kat, whose arm had pulled Todd to a halt, felt a tiny flare of gratitude for the meagre defence.

'In a few years she'll be blowsy,' replied her mother-in-law disparagingly. 'A woman can't use her body the way she does without it showing. Why, Daniel, she practically admitted to my face that she was little more than a common prostitute, and Todd didn't turn a hair! She's obviously spun him some hard-luck tale that he's infatuated enough to believe. She can do no wrong as far as he's concerned.'

'Nothing accentuates the coarseness of a stone more than an elegant setting, Mother.' The soothingly mellow masculine voice taunted Kat with its smug certainty. 'I'm sure a weekend of trying to fit her in with our friends will bring the realities of the situation home to Todd.'

'That doesn't solve the problem of tomorrow night,' continued Adelaide relentlessly. 'She's going to hold us up to ridicule and contempt with her brassy vulgarity. It'll be *us* she embarrasses; I doubt if she knows the meaning of the word herself.'

'Let's get through dinner first, shall we, before we worry about the rest of the weekend?' Her son sounded insufferably bored by the whole subject, and Kat disliked him all the more. 'Perhaps she'll find your efforts tonight sufficiently daunting to realise the futility of trying to gatecrash society. If not, we might have to resort to something a little more direct. There's more than one way to skin a Cat, Mother . . .'

'This is hardly the time for flippancy, Daniel——' Rage tuned out the rest of Adelaide's chilled unamusement as Kat turned and thrust her hand under Todd's nose.

'Put it on.'

'What?' Todd was taken aback at her fierceness.

'The ring. Put it on.' When he hesitated, she put her hand in his pocket and did it herself.

'Now, Kat, you won't go overboard, will you? That would ruin everything,' Todd pleaded nervously. 'They're just talking out of ignorance . . . you should pity them their prejudices.'

'Oh, I do, I do,' murmured Kat, her mind grimly sorting through her mental catalogue of personalities, trying to find one sufficiently unsavoury. 'Come along, Todd. Let's shock their designer socks off!'

'Kat——' Now it came to the crunch, Todd seemed strangely reluctant, which only made Kat even more determined. *She* wasn't afraid of his grandmother and his fastidious wimp of an uncle. There was a personal point of honour to be settled here!

Her dramatic pause in the doorway of the dining-room was momentarily spoiled by the fact that the three people in the dark panelled room were facing the opposite direction. Kat had a few seconds' grace to appreciate what she was supposed to find so daunting: the Sheraton dining-table, centred beneath a stunning Venetian glass chandelier, was set with numbing formality . . . silver cutlery for miles and acres of crystal. Sprays of flowers in the centre of the table and on the marble mantelpiece, and the mahogany side-table with its flanking pedestal cupboards was as stiffly formal as the furnishings. The only sign of frivolity was a clock on the mantelpiece, a silver-gilt enamelled table clock in the shape of a miniature cathedral. But even that was put into diminished perspective by the long, sombre form of a grandfather clock in the corner, mournfully ticking out its measured beat.

Todd cleared his throat nervously. The two women turned, Sharon soft and tender in salmon-pink, Adelaide in a cold blue-grey sheath that matched her eyes. Kat gave them the brilliant edge of her smile, as defiant as the red dress with its bizarre accent of green. But her eyes were on the man who was turning more slowly, almost reluctantly, to face them.

The nape of Kat's neck prickled in shock.

Daniel Bishop was quite as formally beautiful as his dining-room. And he was tall, taller even than Kat in her two-inch heels, with broad shoulders made sleek by the sophisticated cut of his dark jacket. A dazzling white shirt with a hint of silk stripe accentuated the tanned skin and blue-black hair streaked with silver. His waist and hips were tapering, suggesting a greyhound leanness beneath the custom-tailored elegance of his clothes, a lethal grace. A dark wine-red tie and a discreet gleam of gold at the pristine cuffs provided the only touches of colour about his person . . . except for those extraordinary sapphire eyes, now fixed unreadably on Kat as she chided herself for falling into the trap of preconception. This man was no stodgy potato. If anything, he was an avocado . . . sleek-skinned, expensive and slightly exotic.

His narrow, expressionless face was a harmony of structured lines and angles, from the thick widow's peak to the classic jawline. It was the face of an ascetic, thought Kat, noting the austere mouth and cold detachment of the eyes. Or was it? As she continued to stare rudely, a faintly quizzical amusement slid into the stillness of blue and his eyebrows arched with a hint of mockery. He must be as used to being openly admired as Kat was . . . and equally cynical of the effect.

Kat felt a tiny trickle of warning down her spine, but dismissed it as imagination. Why should she suspect a trace of dangerous decadence in that beautiful severity? He was a banker, a pillar of the community, a man devoted to duty, a rigid product of his environment. He posed no real threat to Kat. She was the one who threatened him!

She lifted her head and smiled at him with secret satisfaction. If there was any skinning to be done, it wasn't going to be Kat who lost her sleek pelt!

She flowed into battle. Not taking her challenging eyes away from his, she strolled languidly across the room, her curvaceous hips swinging into sensuous action, the clingy red dress riding obligingly up her firm, slender thighs. The cool detachment of Daniel Bishop's expression didn't change as she approached. He barely glanced at her body, instead it was her face he watched . . . the wide, confident smile, the eyes smouldering with hidden emotion, the 'to hell with the world' tilt of her lovely chin.

Kat came to a stop closer than was polite. That offended him, although the only indication he gave was a brief twitch of muscle along his jaw and the momentary flare of his nostrils as the scent she had sprayed between her breasts rose intimately between them. She was only sorry that it was Colleen's Rive Gauche and not something cheap and repulsive.

She held out her hand in the impossibly cramped space between their bodies as Todd, who had trotted anxiously along behind her, introduced his uncle. She lowered her lashes demurely and then raised them slowly, very undemurely.

'Hello, Uncle Daniel.'

The contradiction of the sexy huskiness and little-girl coyness of her expression had the desired reaction. Daniel Bishop looked down his patrician nose at her.

'Daniel, please.' He fended off her familiarity, then, to her surprise, instead of shaking her hand with distaste, he raised it to his mouth and brushed it lightly with his lips, giving her a glimpse of fullness in the lower lip which was hidden again as his head lifted to its former arrogant height. Six foot four, at least! Kat was annoyed at herself for suddenly feeling small and feminine, the hunted rather than the huntress.

Her hand felt hot in his light, cool grasp and she pulled it free, flexing her tingling fingers. *Fop*, she insulted him silently as she increased the voltage of her smile and repeated obediently, 'Daniel.'

'After all,' he continued smoothly, 'we're contemporaries are we not? We should be on equal terms. Being relegated to "uncle" by a woman of your age and experience would make me feel that my years lay rather heavily.'

Kat blinked at the sting from the politely placed stiletto. She supposed that, from the family's point of view, she *was* in the older-woman category, but in terms of experience it was Kat who was the babe-in-arms, not Todd.

'*Near* contemporaries,' she corrected him sweetly, and judged the placement of her own barb. 'Although I must say you're aging beautifully; I can hardly believe that you're nearly *forty*. Do you use moisturisers to keep that youthful complexion?' And she paid him back for that disturbing kiss by reaching up and running a slender finger along the blue-black shading of his jaw. He must have to shave more than twice a day to keep that dark masculine growth under control. He went rigid at her unexpected touch, and she let her hand fall, honey eyes openly laughing at him. So, Mr Banker . . . so smooth and suave and correct, you don't like to be ruffled. How unfortunate, for Kat was in a distinct mood to ruffle!

'Miss Kendon!' It seemed that Daniel wasn't the only one to find her casual assumption of intimacy unwelcome.

'*Do* call me Kathleen,' Kat said as she turned to look at Adelaide's rigorous disapproval. Most of her conversation in polite society so far seemed to have been spent either instructing or being instructed in the etiquette of name-calling. It was beginning to get boring. 'After all,' she said, with a wicked imitation of Daniel's suaveness that made Todd tense warningly, 'I'll soon be calling you Grandmother.'

'I would prefer that you address me as Adelaide,' the woman replied with arctic stiffness.

'Bit of a mouthful, isn't it?' responded Kat sympathetically. 'You should shorten your name——' *like what I do* was tempting, but a bit over the top, true mimicry never turned into parody '—the way I do. Were you called after the Australian city? I've heard of people being named after the places where they were actually conceived. Were your parents——'

'Can I offer you a drink, Kathleen?' Daniel interrupted the incipient vulgarity, moving over to the cluster of crystal decanters on the side-table. Like Kat, he handled his height with grace and ease.

'Er . . . I'll just have what everyone else is having,' she said gauchely, stealing the classic line of the insecure.

'Dry sherry.' Daniel exchanged a brief, knowing glance with his mother. Shameless, ill-bred, uncivilised, she could see them thinking. But better than you are, my dears, wrapped in your supercilious smugness!

'I usually drink it sweet,' she said cheerfully, compounding her gaffe. 'But what the hell, I'll try anything once. Mind you, this sort of thing is a bit wasted on me. My pal*ette*——' She paused, but Daniel's face remained politely interested and she was amused as his restraint when it was obvious from the briefly pained expression in the light eyes that her malapropism grated. She said it again, just to annoy him. 'My pal*ette* has been seared away by too many years of drinking spritzers out of cardboard casks. I'm rottenly undiscriminating when it comes to wines, aren't I, Toddy?'

'You're unpretentious.' Todd covered his wince at the awful diminutive with a suitably besotted smile. 'I wouldn't have you any other way. Well, Daniel?' He beamed proudly at his uncle. 'Now that you've met her, what do you think of my future bride? Isn't she terrific? And she could have any man she wanted with just a snap of her fingers, but she chose me!'

'It just goes to show that she's discriminating about men, if not about wine,' Daniel said with a breathtaking display of civility, given the provocation. His manners must be bred in the bone, thought Kat. I wonder what one would have to do to make him forget them? I wonder what's underneath . . . man or mouse? He handed Kat her glass and sipped from his own, looking directly into her eyes over the mask of the rim. 'You're certainly a beautiful woman, Kathleen,' he paid her due homage, the emphasis on the last syllable of her name giving it a smoky Irish inflection that was tantalisingly attractive. 'Certainly far more beautiful than any woman Todd has ever brought home before. I can understand him finding himself——'

'In love?' Kat found herself manipulated into providing the words he sought from the air.

'Enchanted,' he corrected her softly with a gentle, flattering smile that put her in her palce far more effectively than his mother's overt hostility. Oh, his manners might be bred in the bond, but so was his arrogance!

He's enchanted *me*, too,' Kat simmered sweetly at him, touching her throat where the diamonds blazed. 'Toddy is *so* generous that he takes my breath away, and so *persistent*.' She tinkled a laugh as all eyes shifted from the ostentatious necklace to the prominent ring glittering its appalling message. 'I know you wanted us to wait, Adelaide, but I'm afraid I just have no resistance where Toddy is concerned. He's so *impetuous*. He wants us to get married straight away, in a register office, but I said "No, Toddy," I said, "I want a real church wedding. Maybe we can even make it a big double one with Clarissa and Daniel—wouldn't that be fun?" ' Not to mention social suicide for the Bishops. Kat ignored the scandalised expressions of horror around her—even Daniel's was verging on impolite repugnance—and held up the awful ring, flashing it under the lights with intemperate glee. 'Toddy let me choose this to match my lovely necklace, isn't he a darling? Although I did think that it was rather small as an expression of our *love*,' a pouting glance at Daniel, 'but Toddy said not to worry, that there'll be plenty more where this came from. Maybe even some family stuff.' She tossed off her drink with a fine disregard for its quality. 'I'm starved,' she announced. 'When do we eat?'

'I think now would be a good time,' Daniel murmured drily, the only one apparently not stricken into silence by her outrageous gall. He pressed a button on the wall by the sideboard and took Kat's empty glass.

'Congratulations,' he said, his hand briefly touching her waist as he guided her to her chair and flicked a white embroidered napkin across her lap with practised flair.

'What for?' she asked guardedly, suspicious of a trace of amusement in his manner, almost as if he was complimenting her on the effectiveness of her bombshell.

'Why, your engagement, of course,' he said blandly, waiting until Adelaide and Sharon were seated by Todd before he sat down at the head of the table.

Kat looked across the clearly defined battle-lines. Todd was almost as far away as it was possible for him to be, next to his grandmother at the foot of the long, formal table. Kat had her side of the table to herself, with Sharon opposite and Daniel's urbane figure at her right elbow . . . perhaps he wanted her close to make sure she didn't pinch any of the silver!

Seth came into the room with his peculiar fighter's rolling gait, and presented a chilled white wine for Daniel's approval. Catching sight of the impressive label and Daniel's nod of satisfaction, Kat smiled to herself, revelling in the possibilities.

A short, angular woman with dark hair pulled into a severe bun wheeled a warming trolley, laden with crockery and a large silver tureen, across the hushed carpet, and began to ladle the contents of the tureen into fluted white bowls edged with a thin band of gold.

'This is just like a restaurant,' said Kat when she was served her fragrant creamy soup and offered a warm roll that could only have been home-baked. 'At home, we usually eat on our laps in front of the telly. Mostly because the table is always buried under everyone's junk.'

'Kat shares a house with some friends,' said Todd helpfully.

'Two girls and two guys,' Kat confirmed, receiving the silent signal. Leaving out the details of the varied talents and respectable incomes of the inhabitants of thirty-eight, Stanton Street, Kat sketched a larger-than-life picture of a bohemian life-style which verged on the radical. Adelaide's eyes, which had sharpened suspiciously at the mention of Jeff and Allan and the intimation of wild parties and general moral laxity, glazed over at the hideous realisation that the Bishops might be harbouring a dangerous Red influence within the hallowed walls of capitalism.

'Thanks, Seth.' Kat raised the fragile tulip glass he had filled, and made a face. 'Where are the bubbles?' she asked plaintively.

'There aren't any, Miss Kendon,' he told her in a carefully neutral voice. 'This is a still wine.'

'Oh.' Kat wrinkled her nose ruefully. 'Then would you be a darling and splash some soda in it to pep it up a bit? I like my wines with fizz.' Out of the corner of her eye, she saw Daniel's knuckles whiten at the heresy. For a moment she thought he was going to snap the delicate stem of his glass.

'Why don't you try it as it is, first?' he suggested evenly, when he had managed to unlock his jaw. 'You might like it.'

'If you say so, Daniel.' She batted her long, mascaraed lashes at him, revealing the over-virulent green on her lids. 'What I'd *really* love is some champagne. You promised me champagne and caviare, Toddy.' She raised her voice with the complaint, pitching it to a stridency favoured by her landlord's nagging wife.

'You'll get plenty of both tomorrow night,' Todd told her fondly. 'Dom Pérignon and best Beluga.'

'Both somewhat over-rated, Kathleen,' Daniel remarked cynically, the beautiful, cultured voice contrasting vividly with hers.

You mean you don't want to cast pearls before swine, Kat guessed. 'Perhaps they are to you. I suppose that familiarity breeds contempt.'

'Oh, I hope so . . . I do hope so.' His voice was silky with meaning. 'Life could become rather . . . expensive . . . otherwise.'

'But you can afford it.' Kat pretended his reference went over her ignorant head. 'You have stacks of money. Or doesn't generosity run in the family?' She fingered her necklace lovingly.

'There's a difference between generosity and recklessness. I don't abuse the responsibilities of my wealth by squandering it,' he said, extremely coolly.

'Naturally we make charitable donations to approved organisations,' Adelaide interrupted sharply. 'The Bishop Foundation, which was set up by my husband, provides the largest private sponsorship of the Arts in New Zealand.'

'I'm in the Arts. Perhaps I ought to apply for a grant,' said Kat brightly.

'What you do couldn't be classified as *art*, Kathleen.' Adelaide shuddered at the very thought.

'Oh, didn't I tell you? Kat's not doing what she was . . . er . . . doing before,' Todd said hurriedly, recognising the dangerous flare in Kat's eyes and knowing how fiercely eloquent she could be when challenged about the one-woman show she had felt impelled, out of anger and personal outrage, to do. '*Stripped* was very tastefully done, but she's agreed to do more circumspect stuff from now on, *haven't you*, Kat?'

'There's nothing tasteful about taking your clothes off in public,' Adelaide snapped back. 'The damage is already done.'

'A little sleaze was necessary for the right atmosphere,' said Kat with razor thinness, valiantly restraining herself from disabusing the cold, priggish woman of her misconceptions. Kat had been very careful in building up her achingly realistic monologue not to cater to the prurience of the 'raincoat brigade'. At no time had she stripped beyond the kind of erotic underwear that could be bought in any chainstore lingerie department. It was the inward trappings of character that had riveted audience and critics, not cheap exhibitionism.

'You should have come and seen me, Todd would have got you tickets,' she added, since they were supposed to have met backstage at her show, not in the respectable environs of the Auckland Museum, where Kat had been helping Jeff set up his part of a display of New Zealand modern jewellery. 'You don't know what you missed!'

'I think we can make an educated guess,' Daniel said, eyes flickering sardonically over her generous cleavage.

'Oh? You mean you're familiar with striptease?' Kat asked poisonously, angry at him for believing every monstrous thing about her that she had led him to believe, and furious with herself for caring.

'Only asset-stripping.'

'My, how ruthless you sound,' she simpered. '*Are* you ruthless, Daniel? Are those horns of yours real?'

'When necessary, and yes, these streaks are natural. Are yours?'

Kat tossed her sun-streaked locks. 'If you'd come to my play, you wouldn't have to ask that question,' she taunted.

. He picked up the gauntlet with extravagant ease. 'I'm afraid I have to pick and choose my social engagements fairly carefully,' he drawled. 'I have a very low boredom threshold.'

Kat was torn between laughter and rage. What class! So cool . . . so calm . . . so polite. So insulting! Admiration won, and her eyes melted into liquid pools of eighteen-carat amusement.

'I'm crushed,' she said gravely, trying to make her helplessly laughing eyes as deadpan as her face while he regarded her thoughtfully through narrowed lids. She could feel Todd's concern filtering the length of the table, and knew that she couldn't keep flirting with Daniel's intelligence indefinitely, in spite of the pleasure it gave her . . . or perhaps because of it.

For the rest of the sumptuously stately meal Kat devoted herself to doing justice to the superb food, but even there she managed to reveal her lack of breeding. Her genuine, uninhibitedly sensual appreciation of dish after dish of delights was apparently just as gauche as her wickedly creative approach to cutlery. Impervious to Adelaide's attempts to maintain the elevated tone of the long-drawn-out proceedings with highbrow conversation and pointed remarks about the impropriety of attacking one's fish with one's fruit fork, Kat made an enjoyable hash of her own table setting and then began filching from Daniel's.

'I'm stuffed!' she announced after licking the last blissful morsel of Black Forest cherry cake from her stolen dessert spoon with a blatantly erotic stroke of her tongue which made the apparently relaxed man at the head of the table momentarily lose his inscrutable detachment and wonder heatedly what other, more pleasurable skills that agile tongue could perform. 'Mmm. I can't wait to eat like this every night!'

'We usually eat far more simply than this,' Adelaide said repressively, although her idea of simple was no doubt far different from Kat's. 'Mrs Smythe made a special effort this evening.'

'Really? You mean all of this was just for *me*?' Kat smugly misinterpreted Adelaide's object as she surveyed the ruins of the beautiful meal. 'You don't know what a relief that is! And to think that Toddy and I were worried that you were going to try and make things difficult for us. Why, after this fabulously impressive welcome, I feel almost part of the family already!'

Adelaide, the tables neatly turned, looked as if she had swallowed a sour cherry. Every arrow she had launched had been deflected by her target's rhinoceros-like insensitivity.

Kate punctured the yawning silence with a yawn of her own, wide and jaw-cracking.

'Sorry.' She grinned unapologetically. 'I haven't got to bed before dawn any night this week, and it's beginning to catch up with me.' No need to mention that she had been working at Gino's all-night restaurant and not been out carousing on the tiles. She pushed her chair back and stood up and stretched with unselfconscious pleasure at her sense of weary physical well-being. 'I hate to eat and run, but I'm bushed. I think I'll go up to my room and crash before I pass out under the table. No coffee, thanks, Mrs Smythe.' She waved the woman away with an elegantly friendly smile. 'Though I'm sure it's as sublime as the food. Coming, Toddy?'

'*Todd* will remain until we have finished dining,' said Adelaide frigidly, underlining with a silent look the incredible rudeness of her uninvited guest. 'There is some family business to discuss.'

I bet! Kat grinned at Todd's hunted look. The fact that this was all a charade wasn't going to make his ride any less rough.

'You really shouldn't lie down so soon after a big meal. You should get a little exercise first,' Sharon Bishop offered her first real opinion of the evening in her soft, meek voice. Kat smiled at her kindly. Kat felt sorry for her, in spite of her wealth and luxurious life-style. Had she been as self-effacing when Sean Bishop was alive, or was it ten years of widowhood in the shadow of her mother-in-law's cold, dominating personality that had turned her into a cipher?

'Oh, I never exercise.' Her voice had unconsciously softened, the way everyone's did when they spoke to Sharon.

'Never?' Daniel's involuntary remark was drily sceptical.

Kat looked down at her superb body. 'Well, what I do for exercise most people don't call exercise, if you know what I mean,' she said, giving him a sly wink.

'You could hardly be more explicit.'

'Oh, yes, I could. I can be very, *very* much more explicit.' She could, for instance, tell them that slaving away in the steamy, bustling family atmosphere of Gino's kitchen for seven hours a night would maintain a body-builder's muscle tone! 'Big, juicy scenes are something I've had a *lot* of practice at.' And with that warning she strolled around the table to give Todd a generous, encouraging kiss full on his nervous mouth. 'Until later, darling,' she said with sulty significance, and prepared to make her triumphant exit.

Daniel was there before her, opening the door with a casual politeness that suggested such small acts of courtesy were second nature. A lady must be treated like a lady, even if she refused to behave like one. Poor Daniel. He, too, was a prisoner, a captive of convention.

She made a tiny growling sound in the back of her throat as she deliberately brushed her body past his, her eyes glistening with honey-gold derision at his rigidity. 'Night, Tiger,' she purred suggestively and went out, chuckling lazily at the inappropriateness of that mocking appelation.

It was lucky for her peace of mind that she didn't look back. The eyes that followed her were neither casual not polite. Black pupils, surrounded by ice-blue, smouldered with a dark sexual radiance, purely male and purely insolent, hot and sweet, a counterpoint to the cynical smile of appreciation on the faintly cruel line of his mouth.

He waited for the soft sting in his loins to subside before

he turned back to the room. Kat Kendon's frank sensuality exerted a primitive, earthy appeal that was too overpowering for Daniel's refined taste. He preferred his women with a cool, subtle touch of mystery. And yet she had managed to jolt his dormant libido into unexpected life with her flagrantly obvious trick. She was even more brazen than Adelaide described, and quite as impossible. While he now had some inkling of the kind of fascination that she held for his nephew, he was confident that the very attributes that Todd found so exciting—her bold disregard for social restraint, her almost voluptuous self-absorption and the childlike greed that demanded instant gratification of her appetites—would prove her downfall. It was a pity that such beauty was corrupt, but that being so, Daniel had no compunction about furthering that corruption . . .

CHAPTER THREE

A VAGUE sound invaded Kat's sun-induced lassitude. She ignored it, disposing her long, golden limbs more comfortably on the padded poolside lounger. This was the life! Nothing more taxing on her mind but whether or not she should bestir herself from sinful sloth for a pre-lunch swim.

She had found the silk sheets and shamefully soft bed addictive, and had blotted her new day's copybook while still unconscious by not turning up for breakfast. Todd had woken her eventually, with a groaning tray, and had perched on her bed to share her coffee as he had entertained her with edited highlights of the previous night's family conclave. She had laughed at being labelled a brass-plated fortune hunter by Adelaide, but her smile had thinned when Todd had blithely repeated Daniel's advice to . . . 'slow down a little, give yourself time to enjoy the relationship before you start placing restrictions on it'. Translation: bed her but don't wed her.

The sound came again, this time accompanied by a light touch on her shoulder that made her swat at it lazily, smiling without opening her eyes as she encountered a masculine hand. Todd must be back. He and Daniel had had to go into the office for an hour or so.

'No try before you buy,' she admonished teasingly.

'Is that an invitation to bid?'

Her eyes flew open, then narrowed against the light which angled in under the sun umbrella shading her head and shoulders. Daniel Bishop stood beside the pool, the dryness of his voice reflected in the sardonic expression on the handsome face. He was wearing a buttermilk polo shirt and fawn trousers pleated softly against the flatness of his waist.

A lizardskin belt and shoes completed the picture of crisp, studied casualness. He looked as if he had just stepped out of a Geoffrey Beene advertisement in the *New York Times* colour supplements that Kat's dentist used to distract waiting patients from the ordeal ahead.

'I thought you were Todd.'

An eyebrow rose, intensifying the sardonic expression. 'No wonder the boy is so jumpy. Are you still at the bargaining table? I rather got the impression when I passed your bedroom this morning that Todd had already exercised his option.'

'Did you?' she murmured witlessly, her brain still too sluggish to admire his insulting extension of the metaphor.

Daniel had chosen the perfect moment to glance in her half-open door as he strode down the hallway with his briefcase. Kat had been laughing at something Todd had said and he, having whisked the depleted breakfast tray on to the floor, had been kindly anchoring the slippery silk over her shaking shoulders. From the hallway it had probably looked anything but the brotherly, affectionate gesture it had been. There hadn't even been a whisper of lechery in Todd's grin.

The sleepy blinking of her sun-gold eyes reminded Daniel very vividly of how she had looked, tousled and flushed and utterly sensual in the midst of the sweet disorder of her bed. It was obvious to him what the two of them had been doing on the bed, and he had felt another irrational, distasteful stab of desire. He had parried it by acknowledging it as a purely physical response, unconnected to the powerful intellect that ruled his life. Intellectually, Kat Kendon left him cold. Even if he bedded her, and she lived up to the sultry promise that enveloped her like a mist, he knew he would find the experience unsatisfying. Maturity had refined the appetites of his youth. He was still highly sexed, an imaginative lover with a taste for experimentation, but these days he demanded more of himself and his partner than mere pleasure. He required the mental stimulation of a woman's mind as well as the physical stimulation of her body to sustain his interest and arousal.

That was what made Clarissa such a perfect choice as his mate. She shared his fastidiousness. She was cool, composed and cultivated, and her ambitions perfectly reflected his own. As yet their physical intimacy had been limited, but Daniel felt no urgency on that score, he had never yet disappointed a woman in bed. Marriage would require only a small personal adjustment in each of their lives.

The thought soothed him, allowing him the luxury of admiring the near nudity of the woman spread out before him from the safety of his complacency.

A complacency that was immediately challenged as Kat moved restlessly under his unreadable gaze. 'Did Todd come back with you?' she asked, her body flexing and tautening as she turned to look back at the house. The fine pores of her honey-gold skin exuded a faint dew of sweat which highlighted the ripple of supple flesh over a magnificent bone-structure.

'Something came up. He'll be longer than he expected. He asked me to tender his apologies.' From the grim satisfaction in his voice, Kat guessed that Daniel had been responsible for the 'something'. He was frowning, though, his arrogant mouth tight, as if he had suddenly confronted some new, unpleasant complication. Kat steamed. How dared he look at her with that cold haughtiness, as if he was an art appraiser who was studying a particularly beautiful piece of art, but a forgery none the less, and thus, in his eyes, worthless?

With mock coyness Kat bent her knee, drawing his eyes to the minuscule triangle tied cunningly at her luscious hips. She had never felt ashamed of her body, and she wasn't about to be intimidated into it now. 'Do you like it? Actually, this isn't a bikini at all.' She unnecessarily hitched up the red and purple bandeau strip binding her ripe breasts. 'It's two scarves. I'm afraid Todd forgot to tell me to pack a swimsuit.'

'He could have offered you one from here,' Daniel replied curtly. 'We have plenty of spares available for guests.'

'I didn't decide that I wanted a swim until he had left.

Besides, I don't see anything wrong with this, do you?'

'You mean, besides the fact that it barely exists at all?'

'Oh, don't be such a prude, Daniel,' she pouted, disappointed that his tone had been dry rather than condemning. 'All the important bits are covered; I don't see how anyone could be offended. Why should I hide my light under a bushel? If you've got it, flaunt it, that's my motto.'

'I never would have guessed,' he said ironically. 'I'm not a prude, but I don't happen to find blatant exposure particularly attractive.'

'Ah,' Kat nodded sagely. 'You like your sex dressed up. I bet you insist on having the lights off, too. Or do you close your eyes in case you see anything nasty? How do you know you're not asleep? How does *she* know?' She laughed, exhilarated by the brief flash of temper that penetrated his coolness, and the novelty of saying such wicked things with impunity. He was asking to be shocked.

'I'm very articulate. I tell her.'

'W . . . what?' Kat's laughter died in her throat. Her eyes widened on his bland face.

'I like to describe what I'm doing, and what it feels like, and what I want her to feel,' he continued in the same soft, measured voice. 'Most women find it . . . instructive . . . as well as arousing. I don't, however, talk in my sleep.'

Kat looked away from the strange, glittering light in his eyes and managed a nervous laugh, still not altogether sure that the indecently erotic words hadn't been generated by her own sun-fevered brain. While she scrabbled for a suitably blasé reply, Daniel quelled a childishly cocky impulse to rock on his heels and said smoothly, in a brisk and ordinary tone, 'Even if you're wearing a screen you can burn, especially in the heat of the day. You should cover up for that reason alone.'

'You . . . I never burn, it must be my gypsy ancestry,' she said, a weak attempt at her former provocativeness.

There wasn't even a nibble. 'Prolonged exposure to ultra-violet rays can cause irreparable damage to your skin,

whether it actually reddens or not. You wouldn't want that
soft, flawless honey-sweet skin to become leathery and
wrinkled before its time, would you? Premature ageing and
skin cancer are high prices to pay for the sake of a fashionable
tan.'

His cool concern caused several faint after-shocks. 'Soft,
flawless, honey-sweet' . . . why did she find his words
threatening rather than flattering? 'I'm very articulate' . . .
what kind of things *did* he whisper to a woman in the
extremities of passion? Kat shivered at the undesirable
splinter of curiosity that embedded itself in her
consciousness.

'I don't think I'm in too much danger. I tan quickly, but I
don't spend a lot of time just lolling in the sun. I'm a working
girl, remember,' unconsciously using a slang term that
confirmed his worst opinion, 'a night-owl. I'm usually asleep
in the middle of the day . . . at least, that was the routine until
Toddy came along and swept me off my feet. The darling
won't *hear* of me working after we're married, so I could
suppose you could say I'm getting in practice for a life of
lovely idleness.' She backed up her lazy smile with a languid
wave at the frosted glass jug of juice and stack of magazines
on the table beside her.

She'd had no qualms about coming out to laze beside the
pool while Adelaide and Sharon directed the army of workers
who had invaded the house to prepare it for the celebrations
ahead. That was their job and one that didn't interest Kat at
all. Besides, her own had been done so well that she knew
any offer of help on her part would have been greeted with
horror. The social leper must be kept quarantined as long as
possible, so as not to contaminate the hired help as well as the
guests . . .

'All the more reason to be careful. When you depend on
youth and beauty for your livelihood, it would be foolish to
sabotage your investment by too much of a good thing.'

'I do have other attributes,' she rebuked him.

'Sexual expertise?' he said smoothly. 'An over-valued

commodity in the market-place, with a high depreciation value.'

'I hope Clarissa agrees with you, or you could be in for some problems yourself.' Kat struggled with her temper, wishing he would drop the pompous financial metaphors and use a little honest-to-good frankness. But, of course, that would be in bad taste! 'Would you like me to have a woman-to-woman chat with her?' she offered wickedly. 'Give her some tips? If we're going to be sisters-in-law——'

'That's very much open to question,' he said brutally.

'*Danny*!' Kat sat up, rounding her lovely eyes with gleeful awe. 'You're *not* thinking of *jilting* her, are you? On the very *eve* of your *engagement*?'

'I was referring to you and Todd,' he said caustically. 'And my name is not, and never will be, Danny. This propensity of yours for nauseating nicknames is extremely irritating——'

'Swallowed a dictionary, Dan-i-el?' For one delicious moment she thought he was going to explode into an elegant display of fireworks. But suddenly his eyes narrowed, a shrewd speculation sliding into the cool depths.

'Are you *trying* to be offensive, Kathleen?'

Uh-oh! 'Purely accidental. I was only teasing.' She pouted prettily. 'Doesn't anyone ever tease you, Daniel?'

'Only good friends.' Making it clear that she would never fit into that category.

'Not family?' she enquired syrupily. 'Oh, Daniel, I shall certainly have to liven things up around here. When I move in, I'll teach you all how to *live*.'

'We live very comfortably as it is, thank you, Kathleen,' he said, back to the unwavering, irritating courtesy. 'We obviously have vastly different expectations and I don't think that any of us intends to change simply to accommodate your idea of entertainment.'

'*I* expect to be happy, that's all. What about you? What do you wish for most in the world? What secret and forbidden desires lurk in your banker's breast?'

'And rich, don't forget rich,' he said cynically, ignoring her provocative question.

'Money can't buy happiness, Daniel, even *I* realise that,' she said impatiently. If only he knew how little she envied him. 'If it did, your mother would be a vessel of sweetness and light instead of a joyless wet blanket.'

His head went up as if she had clipped him on the jaw, his nostrils flaring. 'You will do Adelaide the courtesy of behaving like a guest, and refrain from abusing her hospitality behind her back.'

'Hospitality? Huh!' Kat's temper finally got the better of her. She rolled off the sun-lounger and hit the ground moving. She squared off in front of him, glad of the height that made it possible for her to toss her tawny head and sizzle him comfortably in the eye. To hell with beating about the bush! 'Why should I behave like a guest when I'm treated like some stray dog Todd's dragged in off the street?'

'Cat,' he corrected involuntarily, uncomfortably aware of the tigerish beauty confronting him, the aggressive stance of the long, naked legs, heaving golden breasts, hair flaring sun-red, tossed back over the nude slope of her shoulders, eyes blazing with a contemptuous pride that caught him by surprise. He summoned the formidable defence of his brain to counteract the savage impulse to crush that lovely defiance with a primitive display of physical, rather than intellectual force. 'You have been shown every courtesy——'

'*Cold* courtesy,' Kat interrupted. 'Show the dumb little tramp that she doesn't belong by overwhelming her with inadequacy. Adelaide has done everything she can to make me feel out of place, but she's not going to succeed. Do you know why? Because she can't despise me any more than I despise her, for trying to relive her life by manipulating others. I may not have her *ladyship's* airs and graces, but I'd rather be a woman than a lady any day, if being a lady is dependent more on whether you use the "right" fork, or the "right" grammar, than whether you're capable of love or common human compassion!' She was in full, glorious flight now, and enjoying it. 'If you think I can be frightened off by your mealy-mouthed hypocrisy, think again, mister! I learnt the hard way to hold what I have, and make no mistake, I have Todd. I'm not about to slink meekly away with my tail between my legs just so he can marry some prissy little débutante Adelaide has lined up for him, and if you try any funny business I think Todd might surprise you. He's not like you, you see.' She stepped back and looked him up and down, winding up for the big finish. 'Todd's not some wimp in designer clothes masquerading as a man, he's not about to let Adelaide or you or his mother, or your damned bank, run his life for him. He's going to forge his own destiny, with my help, and there's not a damned thing you can do about it! And don't hold out any big hopes that he'll get tired of me, given time. There've been a lot of men in my life, Danny boy, and I can truthfully say that not one of them ever lost interest before *I* wanted him to!'

They had stormed off in frustrated rage, walked out with egos pricked and lecherous hopes dashed, but never, never with a yawn!

Satisfied with his stunned expression, Kat turned and dived gracefully into the silken blue water at their feet, a fine gesture of carelessness somewhat spoiled by the fact that the dive pulled her makeshift bikini awry and she nearly drowned trying to wrestle it back into place before she surfaced.

When she finally came up she was laughing ruefully, coughing up water. 'Rats!' she spluttered as she swam over to the side. 'My grand exit ruined! I shall graciously permit you to gloat and admit that I should have worn something more . . . substantial for a swim.'

Daniel was taken aback by the swift, but transparently genuine switch from fiery pride to humble self-derision. It implied a complexity that he had not thought her shallow mind capable of. Then, too, he was still trying to adjust to the astonishing vision of himself as a wimp. Daniel had been called many things in his time, but not even his worst enemies had ever accused him of being effete, or cast aspersions on his manhood. This brazen hussy had dared both in the same breath, with every appearance of conviction! Was that why she had looked so shocked at his impulsive response to her goading about his sexual technique? He found the notion insulting in the extreme, but also diverting. Tempting though it was to offer her graphic proof of her misconception, it might be as well not to disturb her complacency. It left him with the element of surprise on his side, and he was beginning to realise that he might have to exert more effort to shake off Kathleen Kendon than he had anticipated. She didn't quite fit into the convenient category he had created for her in the meticulous scheme of things, and that was disconcerting, to say the least . . .

'It's gorgeous.' She beamed up at him, the oiled skin of her face and shoulders glitteringly studded with droplets of water that enhanced her loveliness so much more than the outrageously expensive jewellery she had worn the previous night. If Daniel was to exercise his instincts he would dress her very simply . . . or not at all, he admitted wryly to himself. He would be everything she accused him of if he didn't acknowledge that she had the kind of body that prompted male fantasies, his own included. But fantasies held no sway beyond the boundaries of his mind, no place in Daniel's practical reality.

'I can't believe it's so warm.' Kat took a breath and sank briefly below the surface to touch a toe to the bottom. 'It's the same right down. I would have thought that a pool this long and deep would stay quite cool.'

'It's solar-heated. There are panels along the cabana roofs.' Daniel nodded towards the neat row of slope-roofed blue and white changing cubicles at the far end of the pool. 'They maintain the water at about thirty degrees centigrade in summer, warmer in winter when there's supplementary electrical back-up.'

'Delicious.' She might have known there was a reason that they didn't have a spa pool. It would have been superfluous with a heated pool, and jacuzzis in all the en suite bathrooms.

Kat swam lazily for a while, expending as little energy as possible to keep afloat. Daniel didn't go away, but neither did he sit down. He stood, hands in pockets, at the edge of the pool in an attitude of patient relaxation, waiting . . . Kat sighed. He hadn't come out here just to apologise for Todd's delay. He had something else to say and he intended her to realise that he wasn't going to be side-tracked again. She dived and came up level with the tips of the lizardskin shoes, flipping her wet hair to one side.

'If your hair *is* tinted and you intend to swim again, I suggest you borrow a cap,' was his only comment as the shake of her head sprinkled the paving stones around his feet. 'The chlorine in the water can sometimes have a catastrophic effect on bleaches and dyes.'

'Like a dog with a bone, aren't you, Daniel?' she grinned at him. 'Rest assured, everything about me is natural . . . hair, teeth, bra size . . . I hate wearing caps. When I was a kid we *always* had to wear them when we went swimming, so we didn't waste shampoo by having to wash our hair when we got out. They always pinched and pulled and looked awful. I guess not wearing them now is a form of rebellion. But then, you wouldn't know anything about rebellion, would you?'

'Wouldn't I?' he murmured, eyelids drooping over the sapphire eyes at her soft jeer.

'Well, look at you—even when you're just slumming around at home you look too perfect to be true. I bet you've been a compulsive neatnik all your life, and rebellion is *so* untidy!' She put one hand on the hot tiles edging the pool, and held the other out to him. 'Pull me up, will you?' It was a command, every bit as imperious as Adelaide at her most arrogant.

Daniel was amused by the absurdity of the likeness. 'Use the steps, they're only a few feet away.' Her surprise at his refusal amused him even more, as did *her* refusal to accept it . . . Adelaide all over. The incongruousness of the comparison blinded him to its warning.

'Now, now, Daniel, where are your manners?' The

difference was that she took opposition in good humour, whereas his mother chafed. 'Is that any way to treat a guest? Every courtesy . . . remember?'

'I'll get wet.' The impulse to play on the prissy image she had of him was irresistible.

It backfired when Kat merely scooped up a handful of water and threw it at him. 'You're wet anyway.'

'You little——'

'Not little, Daniel, that's one thing you *can't* accuse me of being!' She laughed at his irritation. 'Go on, swear. Say something rude and crude. I bet you can't get it past that starched collar!'

Instead he bent down and grasped her raised arm just above the elbow, bracing her forearm with his as he effortlessly pulled her from the water. Her hand clutched at his arm for balance, his skin hot and furry, muscles bunching with surprising strength as she stumbled against him. For a moment they both froze, Kat wide-eyed and wary at the sudden friction of contact. Then Daniel shook himself free and stepped back. Immediately his face tightened.

'I don't think your scarves are very waterproof,' he said in a strange, thickened voice.

'What?' Kat followed his gaze. Her lovely red and purple drapings had moulded themselves transparently to her body, revealing every detail of the firm, full breasts, darkly crested with coolly sculpted nipples, and the lushly shadowed V between her thighs.

Kat felt the colour whip into her cheeks.

'I thought gentlemen didn't stare,' she snapped, hands itching to cover her modesty in a betraying gesture of innocence.

His eyes rose to her face, dark and curious. 'And I thought you couldn't blush.'

'Then we were both wrong, weren't we?'

'So you are capable of feeling shame,' he murmured with satisfaction, and she reacted fiercely.

'I have nothing to be ashamed of.'

'Did you blush on stage? When all those men in the audience watched you strip to your skin, touched you with their eyes?'

'It wasn't like that——' She couldn't defend herself without blowing her cover. 'I . . . that was different,' she said lamely.

'Yes. *This* is real life and real life can be infinitely more complicated and unpleasant. In real life one has to face the consequences of one's past actions, however unwelcome. It isn't a game where you can cheat with impunity if you don't like the rules. I'm very much afraid that the only person who is going to get hurt in this situation is you, Kathleen. Do you love my nephew?'

She was unprepared for the bald question, and it showed.

'I thought not. He *will* realise it, Kathleen, for all your cleverness and beauty and skill. He won't be blind forever, and we Bishops treat betrayal harshly. I think you'll find that you don't know Todd half as well as you boast you do. How can you? The world that has shaped him and the world that you come from are totally different . . . too different. You have far more to lose in this than any of us, because you have further to fall.'

'Is that a threat?' Kat turned away and picked up the huge fluffy towel that she had brought from her bathroom. She didn't trust the soft seriousness of his logic. He was being almost . . . gentle, as he attempted to strip her of her dignity.

'Not a threat, a warning. I doubt whether Todd has told you that he actually has very little money of his own. His inheritance from his father is still tied up in trust, will be until he's twenty-five, and until then he is on an allowance at the discretion of his trustees—Adelaide and I. Nor does he have control of his shares at the bank until he is twenty-five, so his power there is also limited. Four years, Kathleen, plenty of time for the blinkers to fall, for him to realise the true nature of the woman he made the mistake of marrying. And the pre-marital contract, which is a condition of the trust should he marry before he comes of age, will make certain that you walk out from a divorce empty-handed. Then there

are other considerations. If you lived here—and I'm sure that
Todd would insist on it—you would live a very restricted
family life. We're not jet-setters; in fact, we live rather
quietly by your standards, and most of our socialising is
business-related, or done for charity or political purposes,
and is consequently rather staid. Social conformity can prove
uncomfortably oppressive at times, even to those who are
born to it.

'You're young, you like to shake the bonds of convention.
Wouldn't it be far more to your advantage, emotionally as
well as economically, to avoid the risk of disillusionment that
can attend the dull minutiae of day-to-day living? Neither
Adelaide nor I would have the least objection to Todd's
generosity towards a friend and lover. Such relationships can
last a lifetime and provide a woman with far more security
than an uncertain marriage. I'm sure you could convince
Todd you'd be more comfortable with such an arrangement.
Think of the possibilities, Kathleen: an apartment of your
own, jewellery, clothes, servants . . . all the trappings of
luxury with none of the tiresome responsibilities. You'd still
have the prestige of being Todd's chosen consort, without
the irksome petty restrictions of wifely duties. Many women
prefer such an arrangement.'

Clever. So clever. Kat stared at the silver-tongued devil,
pouring out his seductive evil. *Now* she knew why the blue
eyes were alight with soft reason, the voice so sweetly
persuasive. It wasn't gentleness, it was sardonic pity. He
pitied her! He thought . . . no, he *knew* . . . that he held all
the cards and only had to lay them out for her. If she was the
kind of woman that she was pretending to be, she might have
leapt at the offer, so generous . . . and so cheap! It was an
insult offered to a fictitious character, but Kat couldn't help
taking it very, very personally. She opened her mouth to tell
him what he could do with it.

'Daniel? Kathleen? Er . . . didn't you hear me call? It's
almost lunchtime. I thought I'd better warn you, the kitchen
is working on a very tight schedule today. The chef and

catering people will be moving in soon, and Mrs Smythe wants to have everything squared away by then.'

'We'll be there.' Daniel turned to soothe the anxious figure venturing uncertainly out of the cool house. 'It won't take Kathleen long to dry her hair and get dressed.'

'Is—is everything all right?' Sharon halted tentatively a little distance away, her hazel eyes darting between the tense couple. 'You both look rather . . . intense.'

'Everything is fine . . . now.' Daniel gave her the reassurance she was silently seeking, assuming a victory that wasn't his. 'Kathleen and I were just discussing what she's wearing this evening.'

'Oh.' Kat had the strange impression that the woman was vaguely disappointed. 'Well, you don't have to worry about your hair or make-up, Kathleen.' Her shy smile made up for a morning of neglect. 'We have an arrangement with a salon.' She named an exclusive beauty establishment that even Kat had heard of. 'They're sending us a masseuse, beautician and hairdresser later on this afternoon, and naturally you're welcome to take advantage of their expertise. And Justine, my maid, will be along to help you dress.' She hovered for a moment longer, as if she wanted to say more, then turned and retreated rather rapidly into the house. Kat tucked her towel firmly over her breasts and thought it wise to follow, before her angry tongue got her into more trouble.

'Incidentally, what *are* you wearing tonight?' Daniel asked, falling into casual step beside her. His question wasn't prompted by interest, she thought sourly. It was just that he was as punctilious about backing up his lies as he was about everything else.

'Red sequins trimmed with maribou.' With mental apologies to Freya's romantic green taffeta.

'Oh, please, not red again.'

Kat stopped dead at the involuntary prayer. 'And what is wrong with me wearing red?' she demanded, hands on fluffy hips.

He sighed, wearing the resigned expression of one forced

to say something unpleasant for the hearer's own good. 'It really isn't your colour—at least, not the shade you were wearing last night . . . or today,' indicating the concealing towel. 'Softer autumn hues would look much better on you . . . wine-red, perhaps, but certainly not scarlet or crimson, most designers seem to consider them *passé*. The romantic, feminine, ruffled look is the current fashion. Who did Todd send you to?'

'He didn't send me to anyone. What makes you think he paid for the dress?' Kat snapped. Now he would be insufferably smug when she wore the taffeta, would think she placed importance on his opinions.

'I wasn't criticising, Kathleen,' he said mildly. Of course he wasn't, he *expected* a mistress to run up hideous expenses! 'Naturally Todd would want you to be able to compete with the other women——'

'Why should I have to compete? I've already won the prize! And I can do without the fashion advice of a glorified accountant, thank you very much. I don't live my life as a hostage to the crazed whims of some ivory-tower fashion designer. I don't give a damn what is "in" for the boring beautiful people. I don't intend to blend into your stuffy crowd——'

'That would be *too* much to hope for,' he agreed sarcastically, goaded into showing annoyance at having his Attic taste questioned. 'But if the red sequins *aren't* just a bad joke on your part, try not to compound the error. For heaven's sake go easy on the accessories, and don't even *think* of wearing that dog collar Todd gave you. You are, in spite of your best efforts, beautiful. Gilding the lily, even if it costs you a fortune, will only end up making you look cheap and tawdry. For Todd's sake, if you have any feelings for him at all, try to use a bit of discretion.'

'I would have thought that you'd be happy to watch me disgrace and humiliate myself with my gauche bad taste.'

'You, yes, but don't make the rest of us suffer as well. Disgrace yourself by all means, Kathleen,' he drawled with that maddeningly sardonic smile, 'but try and do it with a little *class*. If the word isn't utterly foreign to you . . .'

Class? Class! I'll show you class, Kat raged as she stormed up the stairs into her room, practically bowling over the flower-laden maids on the landing. She punched in a vicious series of numbers on the cordless phone beside the rosewood bed. *I'll show you so much class you'll choke on it!*

'Freya?'

'Hi, kid. How's life at Southfork?'

'Terrific!' Kat unclenched her teeth to give her friend a blistering rundown of events. Predictably, Freya found it hilarious.

'One day, Kat, you're going to sympathise with an axe murderer and lose that lovely head! I *told* you Todd was after something, though I must admit that I thought it was your gorgeous body, not just your platonic maternal bosom! But I agree that you can't back out now, not until you've straightened them out one way or the other . . . especially that snotty uncle.' She was less approving, however, when Kat explained how she intended to do the straightening. 'But that taffeta is so perfect! I spent *ages* altering it for you,' she wailed. 'And you were going to tell everyone about this hot new designer you'd discovered. Me!'

'I can still do that . . . you must have *something* that would fit, stashed away in wardrobe.' Kat cunningly hammered the artistic challenge. '. . . so you see, I don't want to be a perfect *me* in taffeta, or dish up the flash-and-trash that Todd wants me to. I want these damned aristos to dine out extravagantly on their prejudices. I want them to be afraid. I want to *murder* them with class. I want something so classic, it has cobwebs on it. I want to be the Charles Atlas of class, and kick sand in that damned *bank manager's* face! Do you know that he told me to my face that Colleen's red dress didn't suit me, and he thought he was being *polite*!'

Silence. A muffled choking. 'Good lord, Kat, you mean the guy had the nerve to criticise your *taste*? Why on earth would he do that? I mean, everyone knows what a stickler you are!' Furious giggles and smothered commentary to background laughter. Saturday morning funnies for the household. Kat brooded on her friends' insensitivity. 'Give the poor man his due, Kat, Colleen *is* a bit over the top with her colours—ouch, girl, that hurt! And I did *try* and tell you that you'd be better off with the yellow.' More giggles at Kat's stentorian breathing. 'OK, OK. Let's get serious here. Fill Coll in while I think.'

Kat spent five minutes filling Colleen in before Freya was breathlessly back on the line.

'Got it! Remember that fantastic virginal white thing I did for Penny Randolph in *Juliet*? She wasn't quite as tall as you, but she had the same . . . er . . . superstructure.'

'Virginal?' Kat interrupted doubtfully. She didn't want to give the game away entirely.

'Oh, don't worry, it isn't any more. I dyed it black for *Lion in Winter*. Now it looks even better. It would be sensational on you. Very, very severe, but very, very elegant. You'll look like a beautiful nun.'

'A *nun*?'

'A nun with *class*, Kat,' Freya added hurriedly. 'A nun with style! A sexy nun! And if my name isn't classy enough for you to drop, drop Calvin Klein's because I snitched the sleeves from a sketch of his in *Vogue*. Can you dash over to the theatre for a fitting? Say, in an hour? I might have to lengthen the waist and hem, but if I get the sweatshop to work on it we'll breeze it by curtain time. Eight o'clock, isn't it? I'll be busy by then, but I'll get Jeff or Coll to run it over to you. Cinderella, you *shall* go to the ball . . . and spit in the Prince's eye!'

CHAPTER FOUR

MR JUSTICE MARLEY threw back his head and roared with laughter.

Over his shoulder Kat's eyes suddenly collided with intense and brooding blue. She felt a tiny, breathless jolt to her system and disguised it with a slow, serene smile. She lifted her champagne glass in a mocking salute to the man across the room. Predictably, Daniel Bishop gave no sign that he recognised the insolent nature of the toast, but the repressed violence of that glittering stare gave him away. Impossibly handsome, impeccably distinguished in the white tie regalia that made most of the other men present look stiff and unnatural, Kat knew that Daniel wasn't half as relaxed as he looked. For all his smooth charm he was a mass of dangerous jagged edges inside. Poor Daniel, rather than eat humble pie he would starve!

Kat, on the other hand, was gorged with her success. Not normally a vindictive person, she was finding the taste of revenge unexpectedly sweet and rather dangerously addictive . . .

The black dress had created even more of an impact that her fairy godmother had promised, thanks to the ruthless pampering of Sharon's promised experts. In a dress that covered her from collarbone to toe, hair drawn back into a severe French pleat that bared the classical structure of her hardly made-up face, Kat looked the image of a medieval madonna . . . invitingly untouchable, more chaste yet more sensuous than any flesh and blood woman had a right to look. The lightly boned bodice with its high, sweetheart neckline edge with twisted black and gold cord emphasised the bold magnificence of her breasts in a way that made the plunging cleavages and slinky, figure-hugging creations around her seem like ostentatious boasts. The sleeves were puffed at the shoulders, then tight to pointed wrists, the low-slung V of the waistline also edged in cord, gathering in a semi-full bias-cut skirt which fell modestly to brush the floor.

The stark purity of the style, combined with her utter lack of adornment, subdued the flamboyance of Kat's undeniable beauty to a dark, secretive lustre that declared nothing and promised everything. She was the only woman present not wearing jewellery of any kind, and for that reason alone she was unique. Todd, after his initial gulp on seeing her, had entered wholeheartedly into the spirit of the game, even to insisting that she take off his ring. He had tossed it carelessly in his palm and then dropped it down the neck of her dress with a cheerful promise to 'fish it out if we need the moral support'.

They didn't.

Kat, the perfect society princess, was an instant hit. During the sit-down banquet for two hundred of the more privileged of the invited guests she behaved with unimpeachable decorum, and afterwards, when the double doors which divided the two ground-floor reception rooms were folded back and the orchestra took up residence at one end, she and Todd danced and moved graciously among Auckland's social élite with the ease of equals, leaving in their wake flurrying eddies of admiring speculation. When a baffled, frustrated Adelaide finally managed to pry Todd away from the side of his 'very close friend' and ensconce him among a gaggle of débutantes, that lady was chagrined to discover the segregation increased, rather than diminished, Kat's popularity.

The combination of French champagne and flattering compliments took their toll on Kat's defiant mood, and as the evening progressed she began to relax and actually enjoy herself, letting her natural wit and intelligence seep through her carefully donned carapace of charm.

There were a number of guests present who had connections with the Bishop Foundation through the performing arts, and it was inevitable that Kat should run into several who recognised her from her work. Inevitable, too, that Kat should turn around from an intense, argumentative discussion on the sexual politics of *Stripped*—specifically her refusal to bare all for the sake of true realism—and find Daniel standing, smouldering, at her back. Kat had quickly ducked away and absorbed herself in a similarly intense discussion of whether the powder snow at Aspen would be as good this year as last, but the damage was already done. Daniel's surveillance had sharpened to a menacing degree, and he had begun to make a point of taking up conversations with anyone she spoke to with more than casual enthusiasm. Clarissa, blonde and *soignée* in white crêpe de soie, glided dutifully along at his side, though Kat couldn't help noticing out of the corner of her eye that she was giving her fiancé a few puzzled looks.

Mind you, Clarissa was a bit of a puzzle herself. Kat hadn't really noticed her at first. She and Todd had so electrified the Bishops with their appearance that for once Daniel's courtly manners had momentarily deserted him, and it was left to Todd to blandly introduce her to the properly starched Mr and Mrs Paine and their coolly beautiful daughter. Clarissa had smiled, apparently genuinely—perhaps Daniel was keeping from her the possible taint to the bloodline in the same way that Todd was protecting his Anna—and murmured a polite greeting that went in one ear and out the other.

Later, Kat had run into her in the large downstairs cloakroom that had been set aside for the running repairs of female guests. Clarissa was touching up her flawless make-up while Kat, who didn't dare touch herself in case her borrowed elegance came to pieces in her inept hands, merely twirled smugly in front of the mirror, enjoying the novelty of not just *being* beautiful, but looking it, too!

They had spoken, casually, as new acquaintances do: about the house and how fortunate, in view of the crowd that was spilling out on to the marble terrace along the side of the house where a string quartet played soothing baroque, that the weather was fine. Clarissa showed no curiosity about Kat, or the fact that she was staying in the house, only a well-bred tolerance of her presence. Kat had the feeling that she would be as polite to a piece of furniture. For the first time Kat was confronted with someone she knew she wouldn't be able to mimic successfully. Clarissa Paine had such a uniquely smooth personality that it was impossible to get a handle on it. Equally smooth, her voice had no distinguishing accents or characteristics. Like a funhouse mirror, one couldn't see into her, only catch a vague and distorted reflection of oneself.

When Todd came to seek her out, he found Kat leaning against the wall outside the cloakroom with a glazed expression in her eyes.

'Been talking with Clarissa?' he grinned.

'How did you guess?' she asked, surprised. Clarissa was still inside, chatting tranquilly with a friend about the exquisitely dainty ring that Daniel had presented her with after a succinctly dry and witty after-dinner speech in reply to the formal announcement by Reginald Paine.

'Your stunned-fish expression,' said Todd.

'You mean, she's always like that?' Kat's brows wrinkled. 'She's for *real*?'

'Deadly.' The wry one-word answer spoke volumes. Todd didn't like his uncle's choice of wife . . . or rather, his grandmother's. 'Relentlessly cultured, flawlessly polite and about as kind as a rock. Remind you of anyone?'

'Why, no, I don't think—— Good heavens! Adelaide!' Kat straightened with a jerk, taking Todd's proffered arm, and stared at him with sympathetic horror. 'She reminds me a bit of your grandmother.'

'Give her thirty years and she'll be *exactly* like Grandmother. Thirty years of living *here*,' he said gloomily. 'In fact, it probably won't even take that long. They're as thick as thieves already, you know, making their little plans. Can you imagine what life is going to be like around here when they adopt a combined front? It's bad enough with Grandmother trying to shape the world and everyone in it to her own specifications, but to have Clarissa sticking in her well-disciplined oar as well . . .' He groaned. 'You know, married to someone else, Clarissa might learn to loosen up, but she and Daniel . . .' He shook his head in frustration. 'There's no spontaneity there. They're so stable together that they're going to take *root* . . .'

'I thought that was the general idea, to fertilise the family tree and bring forth seedlings . . . or do I mean cross-fertilise?' To help her decide, Kat took another glass of champagne from a passing white-jacketed waiter. It might be over-rated, but it was still delicious . . . she really ought to keep track of how many glasses she'd had, even though she didn't have to worry about driving home. She only hoped she'd be able to negotiate the stairs!

'Daniel told Grandmother he didn't want an unfunctional piece of art—you know, a looker with a mind full of trivia. He wanted someone with depth and strength, someone who could cope with the pressures in his life, someone he wouldn't have to "baby" with constant attention. I can understand what he wants and why, but there's such a thing as being *too* strong, don't you think?'

When the strength wasn't tempered by love, yes. Kat had watched Clarissa and Daniel together and seen mutual respect, affection, even, but no visible sign of love as she understood it.

'Grandmother was always a bit of a martinet, but it's only since Grandfather died that she's become really inflexible. He was strong-willed, too, but they both loved enough to defer to each other. When Grandfather died, those checks and balances died with him. That's Daniel's mistake, see—he and Clarissa don't have any emotional connection. Instead of *sharing* themselves, they're going to be living together, separately.' Todd shivered expressively.

'Never mind,' Kat murmured consolingly. 'At least you'll have Anna to stop the spread of emotional frostbite.'

'Who?'

'Anna. The girl you love.' Kat frowned at him. 'The one we're going to all this trouble for.'

'Oh, that Anna,' said Todd hurriedly. 'I was *trying* not to think about her. She should be here with me tonight, you know . . .'

Kat hustled him back on to the dance-floor, regretting her thoughtless prompting. She should have remembered that people in love liked to wallow, given the slightest encouragement. Colleen was constantly in and out of love, and Freya had had her share of broken romances, Jeff and Allan, too. Only Kat had remained immune, protected by her wariness. She had seen too many of the girls with whom she had shared a loose sisterhood at the orphanage fall prey to a pathetic eagerness to be loved at any cost. Kat didn't think love could be rushed or forced. She was sure that one day a man, *the* man, would stroll into her life and spark a mutual recognition that would be too strong to deny. Her romantic certainty had protected her from casual involvement just as surely as her wariness. No man yet had succeeded in even turning her head . . .

'Stephen, Martha . . . I'm glad to see you enjoying yourselves. I know you usually go out of your way to avoid formal occasions like these.'

With a shock, Kat realised that her early-warning device—a prickle up and down her spine—had let her down. Daniel smiled with more warmth than he had shown all evening as he greeted the Marleys, who were still chuckling over Kat's witty remark.

'How could we not, in such delightful company?' the Supreme Court judge replied. 'Martha and I were just telling her how much we enjoyed seeing *Stripped*—although enjoyed is the wrong word; we both left the theatre completely wrung out. Did you see it, Daniel? I know you often make a point of seeing experimental works.'

Daniel, the arch-conservative? Kat risked a look and found herself impaled, her elbow retained in a light, unbreakable grip as the man beside her led Martha Marley into a blow-by-blow description of Kat's performance. When she mentioned Kat's experience as a mimic, as mentioned in the programme notes, the fingers on her elbow almost cracked bone. Before she knew it, Kat found herself outside on the softly lit terrace almost backed into a pot-plant.

'What on earth has got into you, Daniel?' she demanded, wrenching her arm away.

'More to the point, *who* has got into *you*?' he gritted back. 'Don't give me that innocent look. I'm talking about that cheap act you've been putting on. I knew there was something about you tonight, but I didn't realise what it was until just now.'

'Oh?' Damn, and she had been doing so well . . .

'Don't try and play the innocent with me,' he grated as she toyed with the notion of pretending ignorance. 'A mimic! Damn you, it's not enough that you ape my mother's dignity, you have to take the insult further . . . parade even her inflexions and mannerisms as your own. Did you really think you could get away with it without anyone realising it? Or was it just for the thrill of a few cheap laughs? Whatever you intended, all you've achieved is to confirm that even *you* realise that, as yourself, you wouldn't fit in here. If your behaviour wasn't so grotesquely offensive, it would be pathetic!'

'I don't see what you're getting so het up about, Daniel,' Kat was stung to answer. 'I'm far too good to use parody as serious performance. No one's any the wiser, least of all your mother . . .' She couldn't help adding tauntingly, 'The victim is usually the last person to realise, in any case . . .'

'*I* noticed!' Daniel's voice ground out savagely in the dimness.

'Only because you've been watching me all evening, practically *willing* me to do something wrong. A bit of a dichotomy there, don't you think? You and Adelaide terrified of my vulgarity, and then furious because I don't show any? Are you sure you're not exaggerating the offence in your own mind, Daniel? You do seem to have something of a mother fixation——'

'You b——'

'Is this a private argument, or can anyone join in?'

The cheerful query jolted them back into an awareness of their public surroundings. Kat, who hadn't meant to goad him quite so far, turned to smile at Diana and Richmond Rex with relief. If might have started out as an arranged marriage, but obviously Daniel's elder sister had turned it into much more. She wore her contentment like a cloak which enhanced her natural loveliness. Possibly the fact that she had escaped Adelaide's pernicious influence while still in her late teens had much to do with the fact that she looked years younger than the handsome but at the moment stern-browed brother choking on his curse.

Richmond, on the other hand, looked his forty years and wore them with the cynical knowledge that maturity suited him. He was square-shouldered, grey-eyed and grey-headed, with a laid-back manner that seemed to belie his reputation as a shrewd financial brain. Kat had been introduced during pre-dinner drinks, and had been surprised that the pair had shown none of the animosity that the rest of the clan had displayed. In fact, they had been positively welcoming and vastly amused at Kat's reaction on learning that Richmond was the other half of Rex, Bishop, Merchant Bankers.

'Goodness, I thought it was strictly a one-family outfit,' she had blurted, temporarily abandoning her Adelaide-inspired dignity. 'I thought Rex must be the family dog, or a mad uncle locked up in the west tower.'

'The comma fools a lot of people,' Richmond had said in his lazy, amused voice, and they had stayed to chat, seemingly oblivious to the polite daggers that Adelaide was aiming at their show of favouritism. Todd had tried to draw his mother in, too, but she wasn't proof against the magnetism of Adelaide's disapproval and had slid away almost unnoticed, murmuring something cryptic about 'too much, too soon'.

'*Daniel* was arguing,' Kat said, when it appeared that he was going to ignore his sister's timely interruption. '*I* was discussing.'

Something perilously close to a snort escaped Daniel's rigid control. 'Oh, by all means join in. Kathleen thrives on an audience. She's never happy unless she's the centre of attention.'

'Anyone as gorgeous as Kathleen is bound to attract attention, so it's a blessing that she's comfortable with it,' Diana came firmly, and unexpectedly, to Kat's defence. 'You must tell me about that marvellous dress, I'm *desperate* with envy. Someone told me that you said a friend had designed it for you . . .'

Because she seemed sincerely interested, Kat told her the uncensored version—that the dress wasn't hers at all. 'So you see, it's only borrowed finery——'

'How appropriate,' Daniel murmured. The two women ignored him, and he turned to Richmond and began a complex conversation of financial double-dutch that appeared to require his total concentration.

'Freya has her ingenuity taxed to the limit, working with the restrictions that the theatre imposes, but she literally performs miracles. This——' she plucked at the dress '—may have the weight and sheen of silk, but it's not; the theatre company refuses to waste money on expensive fabrics if there's a cheap imitation that will make do——'

'Rather a case of like woman, like dress,' Daniel interrupted sarcastically. Kat merely grinned. Absorbed as he was, he had obviously been following every word.

'Who cares what it's made of as long as it looks great?' Diana declared. 'Really, Daniel, you are contrary. Simplicity and style, less is more, isn't that your motto? And goodness, that dress is a perfect example. I think it's a dream, don't you, Rich?'

'Exquisite,' he agreed, studying Kat with the detached admiration of a reformed rake.

'Exquisite, but hot.' Kat laughed with the same ease that

she had accepted compliments all night. 'I usually prefer comfort to fashion. Perhaps I should have settled for something more summery.' She eyed the extensively-revealed tans on the terrace around them. Diana, too, was showing a generous amount of flesh framed in turquoise lace.

'Oh, no, you're much more distinctive as you are.'

'I don't know,' her husband mused lazily. 'I can't say I'd complain if Kathleen wanted to slip into something more . . . er . . . comfortable.' Seeing that Diana was amused rather than jealous, Kat laughed and gave him a flirtatious twirl.

'Like sequins trimmed with maribou,' Daniel said nastily, intent on breaking up the swift rapport the other three had established. 'Isn't that what you claimed you were going to wear this evening? Much more your personal style, Kathleen.'

'Oh, Kathleen, no!' Diana giggled.

Kat shrugged, wondering how two such different people could emerge from the same womb. 'Poor Daniel, he fell for it like a ton of bricks . . . he's so *gullible*, he's practically a menace to society. I certainly wouldn't like to let him loose near large sums of money,' she told his amused partner. 'It's a wonder that he hasn't bankrupted you by now. One day someone's going to really take him to the cleaners.'

'Rest assured it won't be you, regardless of how successful you are at emptying *Todd's* pockets.'

'Daniel!' For the first time, Diana displayed a fleeting resemblance to her mother as she frowned disapprovingly. 'If you can't take a pleasant part in this conversation, then don't say anything at all.'

'So there!' Kat taunted him, and they glared at each other for a moment, like two children who know they are behaving badly but can't help themselves.

'Better still, Daniel, why don't you go away? Clarissa must be wondering where you are.'

'He can't. He's under maternal orders,' said Kat slyly. 'He has to stick close in case I break out and decide to rip my clothes off and swing from the chandeliers.'

'What do you want from me, an *apology*?' Daniel exploded quietly, in a tone that told her she certainly wasn't going to get one. 'You and Todd deliberately misled us about your play . . . made it sound like a scurrilous piece of fluff rather than a serious attempt to explore a social problem. I suppose you both thought it was a great joke, which is conclusive proof of *your* irresponsibility and Todd's immaturity. You only have yourself to blame for what we thought.'

'And your prejudices,' she pointed out. 'But I'll forgive you your snobbery, Daniel, since I know how reliant you are on your mother's approval.'

He stiffened. 'Keep your vicious tongue off the subject of Adelaide, Kathleen. In fact, lay off her altogether, or you'll be the one *begging* for forgiveness.' And with that elegant snarl he left. Tactfully, neither Diana nor Richmond expressed curiosity about his cryptic remark, or commented on Kat's flush of anger.

'You know, Daniel is carrying it off very well, but actually he wasn't entirely in favour of this being a big, formal affair,' said Diana inconsequentially. 'Clarissa and Adelaide carried the day, but Daniel would have been happier with a smaller, more intimate gathering of friends to celebrate his engagement.'

'Really?' murmured Kat in disbelief. They all watched through the terrace doors as Daniel charmed his way back across the crowded ballroom, pausing under one of the blazing chandeliers to talk to a large dowager in purple crêpe and enough diamonds to sink a battleship. I bet he's not telling *her* that she looks cheap and tawdry, Kat thought sourly.

'Oh, it doesn't show. Daniel is never half-hearted; when he does something, he always insists on doing it supremely well. But this kind of affair is more work than play for him. For all his social skill, when he relaxes he likes to do it in private. Sometimes he shuts himself away for hours with those clocks and watches of his. Typical of Daniel—it isn't enough for

him just to collect them, he has to know what makes them
tick——' a giggle at her inadvertent pun '—and how to keep
them in running repair.' A sigh. 'He always makes me feel so
inferior. Even when we were children it was the same. I'm
constantly starting projects I never finish, but Daniel . . . he's
so damned *thorough* about everything . . .'

Everything? Kat had never thought of thorough as an
erotic word, but suddenly it was. Annoyed at the way she had
been letting Daniel Bishop dominate her thoughts and
behaviour all evening, Kat decided that for the rest of the
evening she would ignore him and just be herself. Have some
fun.

She succeeded. The champagne flowed as endlessly as her
supply of dancing partners, and her casual accept-me-as-I-am
frankness ironically seemed to charm more people than her
earlier dignity. It was a heady combination, and when, after
an eminent soprano had rounded off the late-supper
entertainment, Todd had wickedly egged on some over-
inebriated chinless wonders to cry out for Kat Kendon's
enlivening talent, she was in no mood to refuse. Laughingly
she allowed herself to be pushed on to the low dais in front of
the orchestra, and then proceeded to scoop up her
sophisticated audience in the palm of her hand with a series
of scathing impressions of well-known New Zealanders,
some of whom were present in the room. Soon the laughter
was punctuated with guesses and challenges and good-
natured self-derision on the part of those flattered by being
chosen victims. Most gratifying of all was the sight of
Adelaide, dutifully joining in her guests' amusement, albeit
unenthusiastically, and Daniel, leaning against one of the
narrow columns which bordered the high-ceilinged room,
thwarted in conversation by his friends' constant craning
attempts to see who Kat was going to 'do' next. She played
men as cleverly as women, making up in accuracy of delivery
what she lacked in hormones.

When she bowed to the applause at the end of her
impromptu performance she looked smugly in Daniel's

direction, only to see that he was the only one not even *pretending* to applaud. He had smiled during her act, but this refusal to pay her her due infuriated Kat. He despised her for making an exhibition of herself, however successful, at something as 'down-market' as mimicry. Well, perhaps if she made an exhibition of *him* he would have to laugh and applaud, or everyone would know him for the narrow-minded snob he was!

Her encore was a *tour de force* that nearly brought the house down.

Kat Kendon did Daniel Bishop.

In the small hours of the morning, walled up inside an intimidatingly organised library, Kat admitted to herself that she might have gone a little bit over the top with that last one. He had taken it very well considering, even swinging up on the dais with her to take his bow, although, her bubble-clouded brain prodded her with the memory, her hand had stung for quite a while after he had helped her down, and it had taken one or two more glasses of champagne to warm the chill his eyes had given her.

'Can't this wait until morning?' she yawned, weaving ever so slightly on her feet. 'I was helping Todd and Sharon shoo out the last of the guests. The party isn't over yet.'

Daniel straightened from the desk, which was lit by a pool of light from a brass lamp, and walked across the thick grey carpet to hand her a slip of paper.

'Oh, the party's quite over, Kathleen . . . for you, at any rate.'

'What's this?' Kat squinted it into focus.

'A cheque.'

Her eyebrows rose crookedly. It was made out to her. 'A very substantial one, too.'

'I'm feeling generous tonight,' said Daniel silkily. Kat might have been a little drunk, but she wasn't *that* far gone.

'A pay-off?' She waited for the Dom Pérignon to re-settle in her stomach. Suddenly she felt very, very sober, and very,

very angry. She lifted her chin, like the salute of a foil. 'I
don't usually charge so much for my mimic act, Daniel.'

He was piqued by the reminder. His eyes narrowed.
'Worth every cent.'

'It depends on what you expect for your money.' Her eyes
flamed a yellow warning, twin fuses to her temper.

'You know what I want.'

'Yes, but I want to hear you say it, so there's no possibility
of a misunderstanding, no polite euphemisms for you to hide
behind later.'

'If you insist.' He obliged frigidly. 'I want you to
pack and leave. And in the process I want you to drop Todd
in such a way that he won't even *try* to see you again.'

'Because I'm not good enough for him?' she demanded
fiercely, primed to explode at the answer she expected.

His mouth quirked wryly. 'Rather, I doubt that Todd is
good enough for *you*.'

Kat was momentarily stunned by his answer, then realised
that it was just another Machiavellian twist in his grand
scheme to get rid of her. Did he really expect her to believe
such lying flattery? Her eyes burned brighter, blinding her to
the angry self-derision in his voice as he admitted the
unpalatable truth.

'Todd is still a boy, and you're already more of a woman
than he'll ever be capable of satisfying. You totally
overshadowed him tonight. Oh, I know he seemed to enjoy
it, but no man . . . or woman . . . could remain contented for
long in such a wildly unequal relationship. Todd certainly
couldn't handle a situation where he was constantly in his
wife's shadow. And he would be, Kathleen, he hasn't
your . . . facility for attracting attention, for handling people.
You're too colourful—even in monochrome—too earthy, too
demanding. Can't you see that if you persist in this you'll be
dealing yourself a load of future grief? Take the money . . .
it'll give you far more happiness than Todd will be able
to——'

Ah, yes, there it was, the bottom line. *Now* she wasn't even good enough to be Todd's *mistress*. Now she was supposed to gratefully take the money and run! 'I wouldn't take money from *you*,' she ripped his filthy bribe in half and then in half again to illustrate her contempt, 'if I was destitute and in the *gutter*!' With a grand gesture, she threw the pieces in his arrogant face.

'That can be arranged,' he warned with a cruel smile.

Hallelujah! The detonator! Kat let fly in furious relief.

'Big deal!' she sneered. 'You think that scares me? You think that poverty is the worst thing that can happen? Well, maybe it is to a pampered slug like you, but *I* have friends, real friends, not sycophants or employees or people who suck up to me for what they can get. And down in the real world friends stand by each other, support each other; they don't buy and sell their loyalty like commodities. But I think you realise that, don't you, because if you were so damned sure of the corruptibility of the entire world you wouldn't be so desperately scared of me? And you *are* scared, you must be, otherwise you wouldn't be so keen to shower me with your precious dross.' She reached out and flicked contemptuously at a piece of paper decorated with noughts that had caught on his lapel. 'Or was that scenario Adelaide's idea? Lord, what limited minds you people have. I feel sorry for you, I really do, counting in your counting house, watching your clocks tick away your sterile life, flitting around in your monkey suit exchanging world-shattering platitudes with people as limited as yourself, constantly checking to make sure there's no tell-tale stuffing hanging out of your starched brain. As for the stones you cast in Todd's direction . . . look around your own glass house. First Adelaide and soon Clarissa—your whole *life* is mapped in the shadow of a skirt. I think Shakespeare has the perfect description of you. "Manhood is melted into courtesies, valour into compliment." ' She gave a lightning imitation of Daniel's gracious hand-kissing, camping it insolently.

There was a small, deadly silence, during which Kat tried to recover her breathless momentum. Daniel tilted his head and looked at her, eyes as hot and blue as a midsummer sky.

'Are you inviting me to prove my manhood to you, Kathleen?' he drawled, at his most unpleasantly soft and cynical. 'Is that what all this hectic excitement is about? Bored and restless already? I should have recognised your distinctive perfume . . . the scent of Kat in heat——'

She hit him, the crack of her hand on his cheek sounding preternaturally loud in the quiet library. His head whipped sideways with the force of the blow, and Kat had a bare second to appreciate the tiny welling of blood at the corner of his mouth before he acted.

He hit her back.

CHAPTER FIVE

IT WAS a light, controlled slap rather than the round-house crack she had aimed at him, but its speed and the very fact that it had come at all stunned her.

'You hit me!' she whispered incredulously, feeling ridiculously betrayed. Admittedly she had deserved a response to her act of violence, but *this* . . . 'You *hit* me.'

Coolly Daniel shook out a pristine white handkerchief and dabbed at the corner of his damaged mouth. A silver streak of satisfaction illuminated the blue eyes as he watched her absorb the implications. She looked as stunned and bewildered as he had felt when he'd first seen her in the black dress, exuding purity and grace. For an instant reality had slipped and he had been looking at the shadowed image of a woman from some dark and unremembered dream . . . a woman to possess and be possessed by, beyond the restraints of the imagination, a woman who made him feel lean and hungry again, greedy for things that he had thought he had successfully put aside as a young man's fantasy. The moment had passed, leaving him irritated at succumbing, even momentarily, to the illusion she so skilfully projected. Now it was time for *her* to be disillusioned, and for him to redeem the pride and dignity she had been cheerfully taking potshots at all evening.

'You hit me,' Kat repeated more firmly, cradling her offended cheek in her hand, ruefully aware that it was her hand, rather than her cheek, that stung the most. 'I thought gentlemen never lowered themselves to hit a woman.'

'But then, I never claimed to be a gentleman,' he replied smoothly to her acid jeer.

'*What*?' The cool outrageousness of the remark was like

75

another blow.

'That was just your assumption—based, I might add, on obviously erroneous information.' He smiled, a thin, sensual smile that jangled a cacophony of warning bells. 'As you so graphically pointed out, I have a way with platitudes,' he drawled. 'Chivalry and good breeding and personal charms will open a lot of doors, but there are some that have to be kicked in. In such cases, style and finesse are less important than one's baser instincts, although I don't see why the boot that kicks in the door shouldn't be well-polished. There have been times in this *sterile, pampered* life of mine when no one would have dreamed of insulting me by calling me a *gentleman* . . .'

His parody of the taunts she had flung in his face was perfect, but Kat was too horrified to register it. In the space of a few heartbeats a rather frightening metamorphosis had taken place. The Daniel Bishop who stood within striking distance was still sleek and handsome and every inch the silken autocrat, but suddenly there was an alien, feral quality about him that didn't fit in with the civilised luxury of their surroundings. The eyes were dangerous, the curve of his mouth a threat . . . but of what? Kat wasn't sure, and that was the most unnerving thing of all: the uncertainty. Which was the mask, this, or the other, polite one? Which was the man? And did she want to find out?

'Todd didn't tell you about me, did he, Kathleen?' he said, in a dreamy, almost gloating voice that sent shivers up her spine.

'Tell me what?' she asked warily, tensed not to show how much his Jekyll and Hyde impression had got to her. She had the feeling he was poised to strike at the first sign of weakness.

'I'm the second son, Kathleen. Do you know what that means? It means I was given my head. I wasn't brought up in the stifling knowledge that I was one day expected to take on supreme responsibility for Rex, Bishop. That was my sane, sensible, pedantic brother's fate, not mine. I was free to create my own destiny, and I almost did. I'm very much a latecomer to the bonds of duty and responsibility. I was always considered too wild to ever successfully conform to the disciplines of business, even though I dutifully gained my degree in the subject.'

Kat's eyes widened to their full extent. Wild? *Daniel?* Thirty seconds ago she would have laughed at the notion, but now she was suddenly adding up all the tiny inconsistencies in the man: the times that he had surprised her with glimpses of latent emotion, of wit and a bold sexuality that had seemed at odds with his refined instincts. She had the sinking feeling that once again she had been left wide open to the enemy, thanks to her *fiancé's* machinations.

'Far too wild,' he reiterated, feeding her transparent doubts. 'For a start, I caused a family row by refusing to allow them to groom me for the post of second-in-command at the bank. I was convinced that I was destined to be a leader, not a follower. I couldn't stomach the thought of spending my working life in the chill of big brother's shadow. I think Sean understood, by my stiff-necked old man certainly didn't, and when I turned down the nice, warm desk in the family firm he threatened to cut me out of his will. It was just the impetus I needed. I took myself and my injured pride and arrogance off to Harvard, ostensibly for post-graduate studies, but in between studying and playing the wild colonial boy with borrowed money on the shadier fringes of the American stock-market—because of course all the Bishop money came with steel cables attached—I got diverted from my principal purpose of proving what a financial genius I was. I discovered that I had talents other than making money. I could paint.'

By this time Kat was beyond shock, and she managed not to let her jaw drop.

'I fell in with an irreverent group of art students and found a certain charm in their anti-materialistic ideals. Fortunately it was at the tail end of my studies, which pride and stubbornness dictated I finish, but as soon as they were over I hammered another nail into the family's dynastic coffin by running off to Paris with another disillusioned rich-brat artist . . . female, Kathleen,' he added with black-edged emphasis as the speculation loomed large and obvious in her unblinking eyes. 'I assure you I'm thoroughly orthodox in that respect.' There was that word again 'thoroughly', with all its attendant implications. 'I spent the next few years touring the fleshpots of Europe, living off art and idealism in an unstructured atmosphere of hedonistic pleasure. Only Sean's death and the severity of my father's injuries forced me home. Paradoxically, I think that those years of self-indulgence and experimentation equipped me far better for the job that I've taken on than the sum total of my formal education.'

'Thank you for that potted autobiography,' Kat snapped, finding her tongue at last. Damn, damn, damn! So she had been right about the decadence, too quick to mistrust her instincts. 'But I don't see what I'm supposed to find so impressive——'

'Don't you?' The lie didn't fool him. 'It means that you've chosen the wrong man to oppose. It means that my reaction to threat is based less on my background and upbringing than on the valuable lessons I learned in the back alleys of Wall Street and the byways of bohemian counter-culture. I'm not constrained like my mother by behavioural limitations; if necessary I'll resort to tactics even you might find shocking, and possibly even enjoy it. One of these lessons, you see, was that under certain conditions the causation of suffering can be a most exquisite pleasure.'

His voice was as smooth and cold and bland as vanilla ice-cream, and his sincerity almost made Kat buckle. But she was no snivelling coward, and besides, right was might, rather than the other way around!

'Sadism is the province of the essentially weak,' she declared, conscious that her scorn was a mere pinprick to that armoured self-confidence.

Sure enough he smiled, seeming to lounge before her wary stiffness, yet still topping her by inches, his eyes narrowing for the kill. 'It amuses you to tilt at my masculinity. In fact, you seem unhealthily preoccupied with my sexual proclivities . . . but I outgrew the boyish need to prove myself a long time ago. If my manhood ever melted, Kathleen,' he murmured invitingly, 'it was a phoenix-like consummation in the fires that burn between a woman's thighs, and in consequence I emerged renewed, revitalised and with a true appreciation of the fascinating flames . . .'

Innocent as she was, Kat knew the sudden tension in the room for what it was. Unwelcome, unexpected and undeniable. Oh, no! she wailed inwardly. Not Daniel Bishop. Not this worldly, decadent capitalist who despised her as much as she ought to despise him! A man who didn't have a tender, cherishing bone in his body, she *couldn't* be attracted to *him*! Surely she hadn't saved herself for *him*? And why now, out of the blue, in the middle of a fight, and on the very night he had engaged himself to that insipid Miss Moneybags?

He had done it deliberately, it was written all over him. He *knew* . . . he was trying some of those tactics of his and they had certainly worked: Kat was shocked at herself.

'Your friend is very clever,' the monster continued, following up his advantage. 'In that dress you burn like a chaste black flame, throwing all your heat and radiation inwards. Where does it all end up, I wonder? How brittle is your beautiful shell, how hot the core? How many men have you burned? Could you provide a nest for a phoenix?' He was purring by now, stalking her with his sheer erotic presence. Kat found herself backing away, not even trying to pretend it was by choice. In this case, retreat was definitely the better part of valour.

'Surely you should be spinning this line to *your* fiancée, rather than your nephew's,' she said incautiously as she fumbled at her back for the door-handle. A long black arm shot past her ear to rest on the panelled oak.

'And what kind of line are *you* spinning? If you despise us as much as you pretend, why are you so damned keen to marry into the despicable circle? Do you think I haven't worked out that there must be a reason that you and Todd hid the fact that you're a respected performer? Yesterday you played the whore for my benefit, tonight it's the nun . . . what other tantalising surprises have you prepared for me, and why? I intend to know, Kathleen!'

That was what she was afraid of. He was getting too close, in all respects. She put out a hand and pressed it against the crisp white shirt-front, and was electrified by the tension in the long, tall body that had been exuding such relaxed confidence.

'Don't crowd me, Daniel——'

'The hell I will! I'll do more than crowd. You've had *your* fun tonight, Kathleen. Now it's *my* turn . . .'

There was a rough, cold, aggressive passion in the threat that prompted her to struggle until he put his mouth against hers. The contact burned so much that the recoil was instant and mutual. There was no sound but Kat's ragged breath. Daniel wasn't breathing at all. Oh, dear heaven, *no*! was her last thought before the face above her cleared of its dark, rigid shock and displayed instead a hungry curiosity that swept resistance before it. The second kiss was equally tumultuous, but this time there was no drawing back. The thrust of his tongue in her mouth allowed no polite preliminaries; it was a furious battle for ascendancy, Kat's arms rising stiffly to lock around his neck, her fingers sliding up into the thick black hair at his nape as he wrapped her breasts and hips against his lean hardness. His hands spanning her waist, Daniel suddenly swung her around, pushing her backwards over the thick carpet until Kat walked into the side of the padded brown leather couch half-way across the room. He arched her over the high back, tipping her hips into his until she gasped into the dark, echoing cavern of his mouth.

The sensations were like nothing that Kat had ever experienced before, like a great, exultant leap off a cliff into a black void that smothered everything except the terrifyingly exciting sensation of falling into blissful self-absorption. She had never felt so helpless and yet so powerful, so aware of the body that up until now she had taken entirely for granted. Eyes tightly closed against reality, she flung herself into the shattering abyss.

Then suddenly the falling sensation was real, the hot, devouring mouth following her to the floor as the back of her dress split apart in his hands, the faint burr of the zip drowned by the symphony of desire.

'Daniel——' It wasn't a protest, or a plea, it wasn't acquiescence or surrender, it was merely a word in a void.

'I'm with you, kitten, all the way.' The drugging sweetness of his words was injected into the thick pulse at the base of her throat. Kitten? How ridiculous, the tiny, functioning part of Kat's brain thought. She didn't feel like a kitten, she felt like a tigress on the hunt, pursuing a prey essential to her survival.

His mouth, his hands . . . how could such small movements produce such great pleasure? It was utter madness, utter joy. She welcomed the oppressive weight of the male body as it pressed her into the soft carpet, the counterpoint to the soft kisses fluttering down the arch of her throat and across her naked shoulders, turning into tiny, succulent bites as he discovered the bareness of her breasts beneath the protective boning of the mock-silk bodice. A thick black lock of hair fell forward to brush her sensitised skin as he put his open mouth against hers.

Kat couldn't breathe; every involuntary function in her body seemed to have shut down to concentrate on that single most pleasurable point of contact . . . the soft, slow stroke of his tongue, the sliding rasp of his teeth, the flex of the strong, slender fingers as he cupped the soft undersides of her breasts. When he raised his head, eyes glittering with febrile heat, she could only stare at him, bemused by the sudden storm that had stripped away even the simplest of her thought processes.

'Not so serene now, are you, Kathleen?' His hard exultant laugh shattered her sensual inertia. 'Not acting some self-appointed role, or flinging insults at me, or lying through your lovely teeth. *This* is something you can't lie about. I'm almost disappointed that it was so easy.'

Belatedly she began to struggle, to deny his conquest, hands tugging helplessly at his iron wrists as his hands contracted around her sweetly aching breasts. Watching the frantic passion of her struggles, Daniel felt a bolt of pure energy explode inside him, generating immense heat. Colour poured into his face as a groan tore loose from the cramped vault of his chest, his eyes closing as he bent his head, no longer laughing, no longer triumphant, suddenly as helpless as she against the physical onslaught, a violation of mind and will.

His mouth parted fiercely against hers, his hands on her breasts no longer subtle and skilled but rough and eager, seeking to assuage the need generated by blood boiling violently through his heart and loins. His body moved against hers as if he would merge them through the constricting cloth by sheer force of desire. A tremble began to shiver through Kat's body until she cried out with the agony of building tension. He swallowed her cry, driving more deeply with his demanding tongue, a searingly graphic representation of the act that, in their minds, was already taking place.

It was too much. Awe and fear accorded Kat a moment of involuntary strength, and she shoved shattering temptation away, half sobbing with relief and regret as Daniel collapsed beside her, his breath drawn harshly in his throat. For a few seconds they stared at each other, panting, and in Kat's horrified golden eyes was the knowledge of what had almost happened to her.

His eyes, almost navy in the grip of nameless emotion,

slid inexorably to the flushed fascination of her trembling breasts, naked, swollen, the tracery of blue veins betrayingly obvious through the milky, translucent skin. Kat moved abruptly, in denial of the undeniable, jack-knifing into sitting position and dragging her bodice up against her female vulnerability. As she did so, the flashy engagement ring which had wedged against a seam tumbled out on to the carpet, winking reproachfully at them.

Air hissed through Daniel's clenched teeth at the timely reminder. He watched with savage eyes as Kat snatched up the offending item and crammed it on her shaking finger, as if it was a talisman to protect her from the memory of the last few minutes.

'Do you always turn on that quickly?' he grated, self-contempt mingled with accusation.

'No!' Realising what she was admitting, Kat scrambled to her feet, frantically trying to work up the zip on her crumpled dress. 'I mean . . . I was faking it!' she lied fiercely.

It was such a palpably false claim that it drew a grim laugh. He reached for her back. 'Here, let me.'

'Don't you touch me!' Kat jumped like her scalded namesake at his near touch. 'You keep away from me you . . . you *lecher*! How dare you? You're supposed to be an engaged man.'

'But not a gentleman, Kathleen. I think we've both just established that beyond doubt,' he said, his contempt cooling in the face of her disarray. Anger and desire still rode him, but he had sufficient control on the reins to perceive the genuineness of her shocked outrage. Her height and build notwithstanding, she suddenly looked more like a vulnerable young girl than a practised seducer of men. She had got her zip up and was now adjusting the bodice of her dress with a dismay that was almost amusing. She pressed a hand modestly against her breastbone, discreetly shifting her shoulders in an effort to ease her discomfort, and directed a silently condemning stare at

Daniel which had the effect of restoring his somewhat battered ego. The serene woman of mystery who had nagged at him all evening was glowering like a bad-tempered brat.

'They'll be tender for a while, I should think,' he murmured with mock sympathy, flicking a pointed look at the tight bodice. It was like pressing a button. The red lights in her hair seemed to flare to match the flame in her eyes.

'Shut up!'

She turned her head sharply away, but not before he had seen the quick colour in her cheeks as she lifted a faintly trembling hand to try and subdue the order of her elegant coiffure. Good heavens, surely that wasn't *embarrassment*?

'You're very sensitive there, aren't you?' he said silkily, to test his theory, moving so that he got a clear view of her profile. 'All I had to do was stroke your breasts and you nearly exploded in my hands.'

The pins she had been trying to anchor fell from her nerveless fingers, her hair falling in concealing waves around her face as she bent to pick them up. When she stood again her face was red with effort. She marched over to the small, square, dark-framed mirror on the wall and grimly began to gather up the unruly waves, faltering only briefly when Daniel's image appeared at her shoulder.

'There's no need to be embarrassed, Kathleen. A woman with your sexuality——'

'For goodness' sake, Daniel, why don't you just shut up about it?' she said, semi-hysterically, feeling as if all eight pints of her blood were sloshing around in her head, adding to the hot pressure on her brain. She saw his heavy-idded smile and found it infuriating. 'What's so damned funny?'

'You. The hard-boiled queen of the sexual innuendo and *double entendre*. For a woman of such frank sensuality, you're remarkably uncomfortable with your own sexuality.'

'What utter rubbish!' She managed to grab the self-control that had been so far beyond her reach since that first kiss, reminding herself that other people were depending on her. 'I'm as comfortable with it as you are . . . with yours,' she added hurriedly to the lie as his mouth quirked to reply.

'I wonder . . . can it be that you've never allowed any of the men you've known to penetrate the bold surface gloss to the real woman underneath, the vulnerable woman? Have you managed to fend them off with your games and glib talk? Did the element of surprise circumvent your usual self-control? Is that why you blush like a virgin at the kind of remark that a few hours ago you would have cheerfully topped? Have I shown you that you can be as vulnerable as the rest of the human race?'

Did he include himself in that remark? she wondered nervously. The accuracy of his instinct was devastating. He was far too knowledgeable about women in general and Kathleen in particular for her ever to dare take him for granted again.

'All you've shown me is that you're no different from any other man,' she told him in a voice cool with apprehension. 'You all believe, secretly, that you're irresistible . . .'

'So you feel quite confident that if I took you in my arms again——'

She broke and ran before he completed the sentence, even though she was almost sure that he was merely testing her. With Daniel, she couldn't be sure of anything any more. He caught her, easily, by the door, and who knew what might have happened if it hadn't opened suddenly against them, revealing a startled Sharon Bishop and Todd on the threshold.

Sharon's face went pink as her eyes went from Daniel's cut mouth to the panting woman he held in front of him with one powerful arm around her waist. 'Er . . . Daniel, I just wanted to let you know that Diana and Richmond are leaving. I . . . we should have knocked . . . er—perhaps you

could come and say goodbye when you've finished . . .
talking . . .'

To Kat's horror the pair began to withdraw. She reached
out to cling to the door.

'No . . . wait, Sharon . . . Todd! Oh, Todd, thank
goodness you've come. This isn't . . . we weren't . . .'
Struggling against Daniel's hard grip, Kat nearly fell on her
face when he abruptly let her go. 'Do you know what he
tried to *do*!'

'No, what?' Todd asked with interest.

'Now, Kathleen, what's the point of embarrassing
yourself?' Daniel drawled. No one looking at his calm,
rational expression would imagine that a raging, irrational
beast lurked within.

'He tried to bribe me!' Kat announced dramatically.

The response was disappointing. Todd didn't look at all
dismayed or righteously angry on her behalf. And his
mother, shy, retiring, apparently easily intimidated, merely
lowered her face in—was it amusement? Kat tried again.
'He offered me money to ditch you.'

'Oh? How much?'

The least he could do was act his part properly, thought
Kat irritably at his cheerful enquiry, and she told him, her
voice hoarse with outrage. To her glee, Todd frowned.
Now Daniel would rue the fact he had insulted her!

'That little? And you refused, right? Good on you, Kat.
Hell, I'm worth a lot more than that. If you hold out, I'm
sure he'll up the ante a few thou.'

'Todd!' His misplaced flippancy was frustrating. 'Don't
you understand, he insulted me!'

'I'm sure he didn't mean it as an insult, Kathleen,'
Sharon said kindly. Was she blind? Didn't she realise what
was going on, or did she prefer to ignore it? Maybe they
were both discreetly drunk, too filled with good cheer to
appreciate the gravity of the situation.

Infuriated, she persisted. 'He hit me.'

'She hit me first.'

'When his slimy bribe didn't work, he mauled me!' Her voice rose in frustration. She only hoped that she wouldn't have to go into the uncertain, shaming details.

'She mauled me back.' The shaming details in one, succinct phrase that made her flush, and her tormentor laugh.

Todd's grin was the last straw. Men! She was fed up with them all. 'Todd, if you don't take that silly grin off your face——'

'Yes, Todd, shape up or ship out,' Daniel chipped in with a grin strikingly similar to his nephew's.

'Shut up! Both of you!' Kat thundered in her best imitation of a celebrated fire and brimstone preacher. Drawing the shreds of her shattered pride around her threadbare dignity, she sailed haughtily towards the door and—escape! 'I'm tired. I'm going upstairs to bed. And I'm leaving *first thing* in the morning.'

That penetrated, Kat was pleased to notice out of the corner of her eye. Todd's humour died a sudden death and Sharon, the silent observer, looked nervously at Daniel, the only one to rise to the occasion.

'What a good idea,' he said smoothly, modest in victory. 'I think I'll retire as well . . . it's been a hard night for us all.' And he looked down ruefully at himself as Kat turned her back on the whole unfortunate incident. She refused to pander to his wretchedly inappropriate and vulgar humour, and slammed the door with some force. How *dared* he pretend to be a stuck-up snob, and then turn out to be some bloody *priate* stealing her body from under her without an honourable warning. Thank goodness she was leaving—she would be well rid of *all* the Bishops!

'What do you mean, I haven't got a home to come back to?' Kat's hand clenched on the receiver of her bedroom phone. Her heart hurt and made it difficult to concentrate.

'I mean the guy from the health department says that it's not fit for human habitation until Preston has someone in to fix the drains.' Jeff offered a graphic description of the disaster. 'Honestly, Kat, the place is a mess. There's practically a river through the kitchen and lounge. The place will need cleaning from top to bottom and redecorating. So we're all moving out in the meantime to bunk in with friends.'

'But . . . when will we be able to move back in?'

'Depends on Preston, and you know how he drags his feet when there's money to be spent. A few weeks at least. You just sit tight, Kat, and I'll drop your gear around in the van.'

'But, Jeff, I can't stay here!' she wailed.

'Why not? We all figure you're sitting pretty. Putting you up for a few weeks is the least that idiot Todd can do after the stunt he pulled!'

The very least, thought Kat grimly, although she had plenty of other options open to her. None of her other possible sanctuaries, however, offered quite the space and luxury she had here. It would serve Todd right if she moved in lock, stock and barrel, and threatened to sue for breach of promise if he raised so much as a single objection!

'Well . . . I still want to come back and see the damage.'

'She wants to come back!' she heard Jeff hiss, and there were smothered whispers in the background as Colleen came on the line.

'Now look, Kat,' she said earnestly. 'We all know what'll happen if you come back. You'll get all indignant about the injustice of us being driven out of our home by Preston's neglect of his responsibilities, and you'll collar him to give him a piece of your mind. Then he'll spin some pathetic tale about how his cat died yesterday and you'll be suckered into sympathising with him, and we'll find ourselves offering to help him clean up. No way, baby! Remember that time he, the zillionaire, borrowed ten bucks from you?'

'He paid me back.'

'Yeah, six months later, and only because you got that electric shock from the wiring and he was afraid you'd sue. But we digress. Be ruthless. Tell Todd that if he doesn't give shelter to your homeless head you'll rat on his grand scheme. Remember *Dynasty*—the rich only really respect an utter bitch!'

A few minutes later, her growling stomach tracking down the quiet tinkle of cutlery to the corner breakfast-room, Kat's head was still swirling with her friend's aggressively uninformed advice, none of which she intended taking.

The entire family was in residence at the leisurely breakfast-table, silence reigning as the Sunday newspapers were studied over devilled kidneys and scrambled eggs, three kinds of toast and cups of tea and coffee, constantly replenished by Seth.

Adelaide raised her gimlet eye from the essential duty of the births and deaths column, and said good morning in a voice that told Kat in explicit and detailed terms that her exhibition of frivolous talent on the previous night's weighty occasion remained unforgiven.

Kat, who had decided that the only possible way to handle morning-after repercussions was by applying soothing dollops of selective amnesia, was both relieved and chagrined at the casual pleasantry accorded her by the man buried deep in financial analysis at the end of the table. Such supreme indifference was supposed to be *her* ploy, not his. She took her negative feelings out on Todd, who sprang up to tempt her with the mouthwatering array of heated salvers on the small sideboard. Ignoring her protesting stomach, Kat martyred herself by choosing only some wholemeal toast which she smothered in astringent lime marmalade—with a Fortnum & Mason label—and taking her coffee bitter and black. Todd took the hint and subsided nervously.

Kat sat down beside Sharon, the only person whose greeting held no conceivable undercurrents. Kat felt her tension ease, wishing she could work the woman out. Her gentle resilience was almost as intimidating in its way as Adelaide's forcefulness. Was she the friend she seemed, or foe? Last night she hadn't condemned, but she hadn't helped, either.

Kat chewed her toast, her mood darkening as she tried to ignore Todd's enjoyment of his scrambled eggs. He was acting as if nothing was wrong. They all were, and it was beginning to get on her nerves. Daniel, for instance, relaxed in a gorgeous two-tone knit sports shirt in apricot and grey, sipping his coffee and reading his paper like any other mortal, showed no signs of the demon seducer of the night before. He had no right to look so smugly self-absorbed, as if he hadn't practically raped a house-guest under his own roof. Well, not that it would really have been *rape* exactly, not when the victim enjoyed it . . .

At that moment he looked up and caught her brooding stare. By sheer force of will she stopped herself from blushing, but she couldn't stop her eyelashes from flickering protectively over her thoughts. He smiled, a slow, taunting smile.

'All packed and ready to leave, Kathleen?'

The toast stuck sideways in her throat and she began to choke in fury. So smug, so certain that she was going to scuttle back to her gutter!

'Oh, look!' Todd butted in hurriedly, thrusting the colour section of the paper under her watering eyes. 'We've made the social page!'

There, side by side, were photographs of Daniel and Clarissa and Todd and Kat. Kat just had time to read of herself as the 'bright and beautiful new star in the Bishop firmament', and to notice how much more dramatically photogenic she was than the woman who was supposed to be the focus of the article, before the pages were sequestered by Daniel.

He muttered something under his breath as his eyes, doused of the light of victory, scanned the print. She would teach him to count his chickens, thought Kat pleasurably, adding lavish amounts of cream and sugar to her coffee. She would show him that Kat Kendon was no quitter.

'What a pity Clarissa's photograph didn't come up better,' she said sweetly. 'I feel just awful about over-shadowing her in her own engagement announcement . . . I guess it's just my star quality. As for my leaving, Daniel, didn't Toddy tell you? It's quite impossible. I'm afraid that you're going to have me as part of your household for a long time yet!'

CHAPTER SIX

'YOU'LL burn yourself!'

'Ouch!' Kat dropped the biscuit back on to the wire rack and ruefully sucked her fingers. 'Serves me right for trying to filch one. But they look so scrumptious. I suppose I'll have to wait for afternoon tea like everyone else.'

The redoubtable Mrs Smythe turned from putting another tray of biscuits into the wall-oven of the gleaming, space-age kitchen, her iron features crumpling into a look of humorous resignation at Kat's wistful expression.

'I'll put a couple on the window-sill to cool for you.'

'Thanks, Helen.' Kat gave her the warm, generous smile of appreciation that had very quickly made her a favourite with the Bishop household staff. 'It's absolutely ages since I tasted any home baking.'

'Don't you cook yourself?' Helen Smythe busied herself whipping up another batch of biscuit dough in the commercial-sized food processor which seemed to have been in use every time Kat had popped into the kitchen for a snack or a chat.

'Indifferently,' confessed Kat cheerfully. 'Chauvinism was rampant in the orphanage set . . . girls had to learn how to cook and boys how to mow the lawn. But it was a chore, it was never *fun*. It still is. I'd much rather eat than cook.'

'And yet you sometimes work in a restaurant.'

Kat laughed. 'Yes, but I don't cook. Gino wouldn't let me lay a hand on his creations . . . Oh, I tell a lie, he lets me place the parsley sprigs.' She tested one of the biscuits on the sill and found it was cool enough. She perched on the scrubbed pine kitchen table and swung her long legs, bare

92

beneath white cotton shorts. She had no qualms about opening up to Helen, or any other member of the staff. Family and staff co-existed on separate planes, divided by the rigid social boundaries which Adelaide imposed and Kat blithely ignored. Kat, having been on the 'other side' of domestic service herself a few times in her chequered career, knew the value of making friends with the people who *really* ran the house, and how much they appreciated not having their services taken for granted.

'I work for Gino because he's a friend from way back. His kitchen *is* fun.' She grinned. 'And besides, he lets me take out part of my pay in food!'

'So this is where you are!' Todd's disgruntled face appeared around the kitchen door, followed by his body, attired in a grey suit, white shirt and bland tie. 'Hello, Mrs Smythe. I've been calling everywhere for you, Kat.'

'Have you?' said Kat, starting on her second biscuit. She wasn't going to apologise for seeking out what was, for her, the most comfortable room in the house. At least in the kitchen she was sure of a welcome and a pleasant chat. 'I thought shouting in the house was considered vulgar in the extreme.' One of Adelaide's maxims—intended to make Kat, used to casual communal living, feel big, loud and clumsy.

'Grandmother's not here.'

'I know. She and Clarissa are at some kinetic art exhibition, and your mother is at her chamber music group.'

'You should have gone to the exhibition if you had nothing else to do.'

'I'm *persona non grata*, remember? I don't get invited *anywhere*. I'm supposed to sit here by myself all day feeling lonely and neglected, pining for the mad social whirl of my old, pre-Todd life. Speaking of which, what are you doing home on a Saturday afternoon? Rather dicing with danger, aren't you? I got the impression that without your constant presence at the bank the financial structure of the entire country would buckle for lack of direction.'

'Now, Kat, I know I've been busy, but there's no need to sound as if——'

'As if I'm an irate fiancée,' she said sweetly, 'who hasn't seen her loved one for more than five minutes at a stretch all week? Working breakfasts, business lunches, trade dinners . . . all stag, of course. Are you sure there's *room* in your life for little ole me?'

'As if it's all my fault,' he insisted, very conscious of Helen Smythe rolling her pastry on the marble-topped bench.

'I think we all know exactly whose fault this is,' said Kat grimly. Daniel Bishop was too clever by half. No wonder he hadn't sparked to her bombshell at the breakfast-table that morning. No wonder he had gone so bland and unspeakably civil, assuring her that *of course* she must stay on as Todd's guest until her own home was habitable again. Obviously Mr Hyde was only unchained in the dark private alleys of the night. By day, Dr Jekyll preferred brain to brawn. Divide and conquer, that was his plan, and on the brief occasions that they had run into each other since, Kat had the impression that he was rather pleased with the way he had weaned Todd away from her fatal fascination.

'Yes, but don't you see, Kat? Either way I win. For the first time Daniel's letting me get involved in the backroom negotiating, where the *real* deals are struck —between cronies over port and cigars. I realise he's only doing it to tie me up, but after this he'll never be able to go back to saying I'm not mature enough yet to handle myself. This is a proving ground for me. If I show I can take everything he throws at me and thrive on it . . . well, the sky's the limit!'

'Oh, right, and while you're having such a wow of a time proving yourself . . . how about a similar keenness on the home front? If I'm not seeing anything of you,

I don't suppose Anna is, either.'

The name triggered all Todd's defensive instincts. Quickly he hustled her out of the kitchen into the service hall, ignoring Helen Smythe's amused curiosity.

'I've been ringing her every day,' he said in a low-toned voice. 'But she's caught up right now with music scholarship exams, so actually this all fits in rather well. I explained to her about that photograph of us and told her the truth about what we're doing. She was upset at first, but she realises that we're doing it for her and that this is the best way in the long run.'

'Good. Now convince *me*. Todd, you *promised* that you were going to introduce us. It was one of my conditions for continuing this farce.'

'And I will, I promise, just as soon as her exams are over. Please, Kat, not for much longer . . .'

'Anyone would think that you didn't *want* us to meet,' said Kat, barely mollified. But, remembering the sweat and horror with which she had approached exams—her natural aptitude for enjoying life not geared to the rigid educational system—she relented on Anna's behalf. Todd, though, was not off the hook. 'Well, OK, I'll stick it out. Just remember —I don't have to stay here just because Preston is procrastinating as usual about the drains. If you don't back me up, I'll walk. I haven't forgotten about *that* night, you know. The chips were down and suddenly you were on *his* side!'

'I said I was sorry.' Todd gave his familiar, persuasive, little-boy-helpless grin. 'I was drunk. I didn't know what I was doing.'

'No, but you weren't drunk when you misled me about your uncle. You let me think that he'd be a pushover to offend——'

'I didn't want to frighten you off.'

'No, you wanted to get me good and mad at him first. You set me up . . . *again*. That's a nasty habit of yours, Todd. Does Anna know about it?'

'Do you blame me? Very few people can deal on equal terms with Daniel, and I'm not one of them. I've lived in his shadow too long——' Kat heard vague echoes of Daniel: 'I couldn't stomach the thought of spending my working life in the chill of big brother's shadow.' Daniel had rebelled in his own way. Todd, less forceful, less confident, was rebelling in his. He went on, confirming the thought, 'I'm not strong in the way that he is, but I've got strengths of my own if only I'm allowed to develop them. You don't have the handicap of a family surrounding you with preconceived ideas of who you are and what you should be. You're proud to just be yourself: Kat Kendon, independent woman. You don't have to make excuses for what you are, and that's *your* strength. Look what you've achieved so far. You've got Adelaide on the defensive and Daniel really worried; otherwise, believe me, he wouldn't even bother to *pretend* to be pleasant. In one short week you've opened this place up. Life won't ever be quite the same again . . . thank goodness.'

Kat felt the oppressive weight of his confidence. She didn't altogether share it. Oh, she could face up to the threats of Daniel's wealth and power; they only made her angry resistance stiffen. But Daniel possessed a weapon that, thank goodness, he didn't even realise he possessed. The night of the ball, he had touched her in ways that no man had ever come close to doing, and she didn't mean only physically. His sensual violence, the brutal seduction of his mouth and hands on her body, remained vividly with her. In the space of a single kiss, her sexuality, so comfortably dormant all these years, had bloomed into full and vibrant life. What she had experienced had not been sweet, soft, virginal stirrings of curiosity, but a full-blooded, gloriously intense desire for the full intimacy of a man's possession. Proud and independent? She wouldn't be if Daniel discovered the enemy within!

'As for not being invited anywhere . . . how about coming to the opera with us tonight?'

'I thought there weren't any spare seats in the box?' said Kat dubiously. Adelaide had made a big point of the fact that opera opening nights were a Bishop tradition. The family had a private box permanently booked for such occasions, and there was to be a supper party afterwards at the Regent Hotel. Kat was informed that the arrangements had been made months ago and, although she might grudgingly be 'squeezed' into the Regent, she wouldn't make it into the family box.

'Clarissa's folks can't come. They've been in the States, and there was a bomb scare on the plane they were supposed to come back on. They switched to another flight and that was delayed, too.' Todd grinned. 'The irony is that if they'd been travelling Economy there would have been spare seats elsewhere, but nothing but the best for the Paine-in-the-necks.' Todd had rather taken to Kat's nickname for the woman who floated through life with inscrutable grace. Clarissa had never been openly rude to Kat, but she seemed to view her as a slightly incomprehensible life-form from another planet—an inferior one, of course. Kat had finally discovered what it was about Clarissa that was so disturbing. She seemed to have no sense of humour, no appreciation of the ridiculous. She took everything so calmly and so *seriously*, including herself. She was a temple of reason, a shrine to order. Kat, a disorderly sensualist, was repelled.

'I don't know. I've never been to an opera before. Don't you think that Wagner is a bit heavy to start with?'

Todd shrugged. 'It's up to you. Daniel said you probably wouldn't want to come.'

'Oh, did he?' Kat's eyes began to sparkle.

'Yes, he said it would probably be over your head and you'd get bored.'

'Did he, indeed?' Her militant temper rose.

'He said you'd be far better off staying home and watching *Dynasty*.'

'I'm surprised he knows what night it's on. What did he

call television? Bubble-gum for the relentlessly middle-class mind? Meaning mine, of course. And then he told me I'd make a great television entertainer.'

'I don't remember him saying that.'

'It was one morning at breakfast. You weren't there, naturally, and Daniel was only there to rub it in that you weren't.' She grinned maliciously. 'He was annoyed because I was reading his financial paper and crumpling all the pages out of order. I've got to it first every morning since.' It was the kind of small victory she had to be content with. 'Anyway, I don't think I'll come tonight, thanks very much.'

As she had expected, Todd's jaw dropped. 'But . . . are you going to let him get away with saying those things?'

'Do you think I don't recognise reverse psychology when I hear it?'

'I'm sorry, but I really would like you to come,' said Todd, spoiling it by adding, 'If you don't, Daniel said that Grandmother is going to invite the "daughter of a friend".' He shuddered. 'And you know what *that* means. A "candidate for my hand".'

'I didn't mean you, I meant Daniel. He obviously wants me to come along. Why? Does he expect me to fall asleep and snore? Or join in the choruses?' Still, if she was on her guard . . . and, ambivalent as she was about opera, it was an experience she might regret forgoing just for suspicion's sake: glamorous first night, a private box and flocking with the culture vultures afterwards at the Regent. She had nothing to wear, of course, but that hadn't stopped her before, and it would annoy the hell out of Adelaide. For the rest, she would, for once, mind her 'p's and 'q's and be the perfect little débutante. That would annoy the hell out of *Daniel* . . .

'How could you, Kathleen? How could you do such a thing?' Adelaide Bishop was pale with anger. Kat could almost feel sorry for her—if the woman wasn't so determined to make heavy weather out of life.

'It was an accident.' She shrugged. 'It could have happened to anyone.'

'Oh, no, it couldn't,' said Adelaide bitterly. 'Only to you. Your whole attitude to life is nothing short of criminally careless. I don't know why you bothered to accompany us at all. You obviously have no appreciation of opera . . . you seem to have spent more time watching the audience than the stage . . .'

Why? Kat's eyes sought out the culprit in the dimly lit box. Sharon and Clarissa were talking quietly together, politely ignoring Kat's ignominious dressing-down. Todd, as usual, was hovering indeterminately behind Kat, while Daniel leaned against the red velvet curtain that screened the back wall of the box, ostensibly stretching his long legs, hands thrust negligently in his pockets, brimming with apparent disinterest. But he returned Kat's accusing stare with an expression of such innocent gravity that she knew he was enjoying himself. His eyes were very blue, I-told-you-so eyes.

'. . . it wasn't enough for you that you had to draw everybody's attention by wearing that . . . that *costume*,' Adelaide was winding up to the big finale, 'you had to make sure that your brash insensitivity reflected on us all . . .'

'I thought I had dressed for the occasion,' Kat interrupted, inured to such criticisms. The black halter-neck dress, grabbed off the rack on one of her lightning shopping raids, had looked very flat and dull and . . . *conservative* when she had put it on, so she had dressed it up with fierce red stockings with jazzy black musical notes all over them and whipped into Jeff's workshop to pick up some red and gold enamelled ear-rings in the shape of crotchets. Still something had seemed missing, so she had added a long iridescent red scarf which, doubled and twisted and looped around her neck, the free ends teased out through the twisted loop, sat like a rich, exotic bloom

on her left collarbone. The hairdresser had finger-dried her
hair into a tousled, untidy mane, and instead of using the
Mesdames Bishop's ultra-conservative make-up specialist,
Kate had let Sue, the young upstairs maid, loose with her
trendy box of tricks. Todd, seeing her full glory, had
suggested skipping drinks with the family downstairs before
leaving, and had instead hustled her out to the Lotus under
cover of a white silk evening coat borrowed from his
mother, leaving Adelaide staring suspiciously after Kat's
long, musical legs. By the time the others had appeared at
the theatre, Kat had already premiered, to much attention
and some amusement. Round one to Kat.

Round two was hers, too, for Kat found plenty to
interest her. Certainly, after the first two and a half hours,
the music had palled, but the costumes, colour and
movement down on the stage provoked her professional
interest, and when she had tired of watching the per-
formers she had turned her borrowed opera glasses on the
audience.

Her absorption had led to the knockout in round three.
Spurning Sharon's expensive box of liqueur chocolates,
Kat had instead flashed around her own offering, a
generous packet of chocolate raisins, supermarket sticker
still prominent on the lid. Only Todd had taken any.
Clarissa, on Kat's other side, had looked into the open
box as if it contained rat poison. Having spent the first
interval being condescended to by the woman's ineffable
superiority, Kat couldn't help feeling that it was rough
justice that at the precise moment that her elbow had
knocked over the packet sitting on the balustrade, sending
chocolate raisins hailing down on the stalls below, it
had been Clarissa leaning forward into the reflected light
from the stage, Clarissa's shocked face that the hapless
victims, picking melting morsels out of silk shirt-fronts
and Bill Blass cleavages, had looked up to censure.

Kat, of course, got the giggles, which not even nudges
from Todd could cure. The atmosphere in the box, thick

enough to cut with a chainsaw, had been punctuated for the rest of the act by her poorly disguised fits of coughing.

'Let's look on the bright side, Adelaide,' said Kat, determined not to let the incident get blown utterly out of proportion. 'It could have been worse.'

'I fail to see how.'

She would. 'There might have been no carpet on the floor down there, and I *could* have been eating Jaffas.' The social chasm gaped in the blank incomprehension in Adelaide's face. Kat sighed. 'Those little, round, hard red sweets with the chocolate in the middle? When we were kids, we used to buy them at the movies and roll them down the wooden floors. The real trick was to catch the ones rolling down from the kids behind you and dust 'em off and eat 'em.' The well-bred expressions of distaste around her didn't dim the warmth of her reminiscence. Only Daniel made a sound suspiciously like one of amusement. 'Actually, I wouldn't mind some Jaffas now that my raisins have gone for a burton. I wonder if they sell them downstairs.'

'I think it would be better for all concerned if you remained here this interval,' Adelaide retorted. 'Todd can bring something up for you.'

'I think I should go down and apologise to those people, don't you?' said Kat, moving to crane over the ornate balustrade and waggle her fingers at the milling crowd below. She found herself drawn back with a hand on her arm that was too firm to be quite polite.

'That won't be necessary. Clarissa and I will explain,' said Adelaide, grimly intent on driving her point home. 'At least, coming from us, people will believe it was an accident. One look at you and they would be more likely to assume it was a childish act of sabotage.'

'Sabotage is far too strong a word, Adelaide.' It was Sharon, rather than her son, who came to Kat's defence. 'That implies it was a deliberate act, and I'm sure Kathleen is not so small-minded. Even if she wasn't enjoying herself, she wouldn't try to spoil others' enjoyment; she knows herself how hard artists work for their appreciation.'

Unfortunately, Adelaide didn't appreciate being reminded of Kat's artistic bent. She gave Sharon a shrivelling look that sent the younger woman off to the cloakroom to 'freshen up', or at least escape the torrid atmosphere. Clarissa and Adelaide sailed after her, dignity flying stiff in the rigging, with Todd trotting dutifully behind with the drinks order.

Suddenly Kat found herself alone, for the first time since the night of the ball, with Daniel Bishop. The realisation made her nervous. She would have gone to the cloakroom herself, except that Daniel would probably see it as a total rout. She glared at him.

He held up his hands, square gold cuff-links winking mockingly at her from the crisp cuffs of his white shirt. Kat hated ruffled shirts, but she had to grudgingly admit that, on Daniel, frills looked utterly masculine.

'Don't blame me,' he said, pushing himself from the wall of the box and moving towards the row of chairs beside her. 'I didn't say a word.'

'No, you let your mother say it all for you,' snapped Kat, regretting it an instant later as she remembered where her taunts about his mother had led her last time. 'Aren't you going to tag along and offer your fiancée moral support? After all, she's the one everyone thinks was throwing raisins.'

'She doesn't need my support. She'll no doubt soon have *them* apologising to her for not throwing the rasins back.'

Kat bit back a bubble of laughter as he raised his eyebrows expectantly. She was *not* going to share a joke with him, even when he cocked his head in that inviting manner. It was an invitation for her to put her head in the lion's mouth.

'Although I must admit,' he added when she remained

stubbornly unresponsive, 'I do think it a little unsporting of you to allow someone else to take the blame for your clumsiness.'

It was the right tack. Kat fired immediately. 'It wasn't a case of *allowing*. Your mother was just dying for this chance to put me in my place.'

'And exactly where is your place, Kathleen?'

'I thought you'd already decided that.'

'So did I. I was wrong.'

Kat's mouth fell open. David Bishop was admitting that he had been wrong. She felt momentary panic. Next he would be actually complimenting her on something!

His laugh wiped ten years off his age. Just so carefree and dangerous he must have looked running around the fleshpots of Europe. Kat snapped her mouth shut.

'I'm endeavouring to redress the error,' he told her. 'And this time I'll be more thorough. All I know is that you're something of a chameleon. The only time I get a glimpse of the *real* Kat Kendon is when I take you off guard and you forget to play your part . . .'

Kat froze. 'What part?'

'Ah . . . that's the puzzle. I enjoy . . . intricate problems. I'm very successful at solving them. It's only a matter of time, Kathleen, before I solve you. So why don't you just save us both some time and grief and just come clean, mm?' His silky threat was accompanied by a smile that went through Kat like a hot knife through honey. She was appalled by her weak desire to confide in him, to please him and have him smile at her like that every day of her life . . .

She swallowed. 'Perhaps Todd and I are already married, and trying to break it to the family gently,' she said provocatively, hoping that he would forget *his* role—the honeyed seducer of truth.

'I did consider that,' he drawled, disappointing her. 'But I've had the register checked. You weren't married in this country, and Todd hasn't been overseas for a year. Neither, in fact, were you born here.' He half sat on the balustrade in front of her, arms folded.

'You've had me investigated.' She had almost expected it and, from Daniel's point of view, it had probably been fully warranted. 'Find out anything interesting?'

'If you mean damaging, it's debatable. Appearances, as you well know, can be deceptive. You have quite a number of—shall we say, unsavoury?—friends. You change men more often than you change your appalling wardrobe. You get a lot of stage work but you don't do much to promote yourself. You could be a lot more successful, and a great deal richer, than you are if you made the effort. But you don't. You're a drifter, without ambition, without roots . . . still clinging, I would think, to your childhood insecurities . . .'

'Careful, Daniel, you're beginning to sound like a social worker. I was quite secure as a child, thank you very much.'

'Even though you don't even know the country of your birth . . . your heritage?' he asked sceptically.

Kat shrugged. 'I think the Government and the social workers were always more worried about who I was and where I came from than I've ever been,' she said frankly. 'All I have of my parents is a few faded photographs that were found in the cabins where they were staying when they went boating and drowned. No papers or wallets; they must have been in the boat with them and were never found. They looked happy in their photos, and when I think of them I think of sunlight and smiles, not sorrow. I grew up in one of those small family homes that were only experimental at that stage—where foster parents look after eight or ten youngsters. Of course the parents and children changed from time to time—most of the kids weren't true orphans but were from solo parent families or broken homes, and every now and then the family situation would change for the better and they'd go back. I think that in all the time I was there I was the only true orphan, and the fact that my parentage was a mystery gave me great *cachet*. I used to weave the most glorious fantasies. Perhaps I was a Russian princess,

heir to a Romanov fortune, perhaps my parents were
freedom fighters on the run, or spies! Some of the photos
were taken in Dublin, so the assumption was that they
might have been Irish, but it was never proved. That was
why I couldn't be offered for adoption. They couldn't
know whether someone would eventually turn up and claim
me.'

His face was pale and appalled. 'And they actually
let you live with that constant illusion of hope?'

'Oh, no, they didn't tell me until I was sixteen. I was
moving out then, to board with an "approved" family, and
too busy with my own future to brood about the past.
I made a few enquiries over the years, but I never got
any further than the police had. So just think what you
might be turning your aristocratic nose up at. I *could*
be of Russian royal blood . . .'

'Or at the very least, Irish royal blood.' He responded
lightly to her teasing, but there was a brooding look in
his eyes. 'You're literally quite alone in the world, aren't
you? An island in the sea of humanity . . .'

'Poetic, but not very apt,' said Kat firmly, disturbed
by his empathy. 'I have tons of friends, and actually I
was infinitely better off than some of my "unsavoury"
semi-brothers and sisters. One girl went back to her family
six or seven times, and each time she came back to the
home a mess. It turned out that her father was molesting
her. Poor Nola, she never knew whether she loved or hated
him, and in the end it killed her.'

He made the connection with a swiftness of mind that
no longer surprised her. 'Was that the one you based your
play on?'

Kat nodded sadly. 'She was a sucker for love. Everything
that she did—the stripping, the drugs, the degradation—was
all because she thought that the man who introduced
her to them loved her for what she did, not what she
was. I think she felt so guilty that her father was in prison
because of her that she felt she deserved every bad thing

that happened to her.'

'Were you close?'

She shrugged at the quiet questions. 'For a time. We shared a room in our last year at the home. Even then she was on the slippery slope, sneaking out to see that creep she ran off with, denying herself any self-respect.'

'And did you take a lesson for yourself from her experience? Did you decide that you'd never be a "sucker for love"? Is that why you've latched on to Todd, because he can give you physical security without threatening your emotions?'

'You can talk!' Kat was jolted out of her musing confidence. 'You can't tell me that you and Clarissa are madly in love. Clarissa would never be madly anything, it might ruffle her hair. She's so perfect, it's indecent.'

'Clarissa and I have an understanding. Neither of us have any illusions about our marriage. Todd, on the other hand, has his apparently intact. Love, when it's one-sided, inevitably dooms a relationship.'

'Is that the voice of experience speaking?' she snapped.

He tilted his head. 'Yes.'

'Oh.' With the wind taken effectively out of her sails, Kat stared, wondering whether she could restrain her curiosity.

She needn't have bothered, her expression was beautifully transparent. Daniel saw not only a healthy curiosity, but a softening compassion that betrayed another flaw in the lacquered gloss of her apparently self-serving character. It was like dismantling a jigsaw and then finding that the individual pieces wouldn't fit together again to make a coherent whole. When provoked, she attacked; she preferred offensive plays to defensive ones. How would she respond to a softer, more oblique approach? The urge to probe her weakness was irresistible. The prospect of baring a certain vulnerability of his own in the process didn't disturb him as much as it should have in the circumstances.

'There was a woman . . . in Paris . . . a few months

before Sean had his accident. I guess that even then I was getting a little weary of decadence, because I did something utterly conventional: fell in love and begged her to marry me . . .'

'Was she beautiful?' The irrelevant question popped out before she could stop it, and his mouth quirked.

'Of course.' Daniel moved off the balustrade and took Clarissa's vacant seat. Kat automatically sank down into her own, afraid that he would remember who he was talking to and suddenly put up the shutters.

'Like Clarissa?'

'No, not at all like Clarissa.' His eyes half closed as he watched her digest that piece of information. 'Rather like you, in fact.'

That shook her. 'Me?' she squeaked. 'Is that why you——' She stopped and looked away, biting her lip nervously.

He was amused. 'No, I'm afraid that flare-up in the library was strictly personal chemistry. I mean that she had a similar nature to yours: something of a gypsy . . . very frank and open, and yet secretive, too, reserving some part of herself that was hers alone, never quite giving a man as much as he wanted, or needed. Being in love with her was being in a constant state of turmoil and uncertainty, exhilarating but exhausting. I can see now that if she had married me it would have been a total disaster. I was ready for change, Elise wasn't. She thrived on the high life, on the kind of rootless existence that we had been living. She would have hated it here. When she heard I was coming back to run the bank, she was horrified. "A colonial backwater", she called it. The very idea of responsibility, of permanence, appalled her. I wasn't the man she had thought I was. To me, Europe was fun, but it was merely a young man's game.' He spread his hands. '*This* is real life. This is where my roots are, where I belong. What I have here and now is what I always wanted and believed I couldn't have . . .'

'Wanted more than your Elise, apparently. Maybe you weren't as much in love with her as you thought you were,' said Kat, when it appeared that he had become lost in his abstraction.

'Oh, I was in love.' His eyes were mere gleaming slits. 'I was even, at one stage, prepared to offer a compromise. Thank heaven she was clear-headed enough to realise that it would satisfy neither of us. And I know that no other woman has come close to making me feel that dangerously addictive exhilaration . . .' His voice trailed off to a thready murmur.

'Is that what it's like?' asked Kat, shivering faintly at the erotically evocative phrase.

'Mmm.' His confirmation purred along her nerves. 'And don't think you're immune, Kathleen, just because you don't want it to happen.'

She blinked. 'How do you know it won't happen again to you?' she demanded huskily. 'Do you expect Clarissa to protect you?'

'I'm old enough to protect myself. I've outgrown my headstrong, impetuous youth. One learns from one's mistakes. These days I have more mature requirements. Elise was a young man's fantasy.'

'What does that make Clarissa? A middle-aged man's one?' said Kat tartly. So Daniel considered himself past the age of love. How—sad.

'She'll be the kind of wife and mother who will meet all my needs.'

Kat sniffed.

'And at least I won't have to wonder which of my children is really mine.'

Kat looked at him aghast. 'Did you think Elise . . . I mean, was she . . . unfaithful?'

He smiled suddenly, a gentle smile that made her feel impossibly naïve. 'The word had no meaning in the context of her life. She was a free spirit. We were lovers, but I had no hold on her, no right to sole possession. That was part of the challenge of loving her . . . the constant fight to keep her interested.'

'She sounds like a heartless little tramp to me!' snapped Kat, her eyes emerald with dislike. 'Certainly not worth pining over. I find it hard to believe you fell in love with her in the first place. You don't strike me as the kind of man who would ever be so . . . so *undiscriminating*. You certainly shouldn't let a woman like that blight your life——'

'I promise to live happily ever after,' he vowed gravely, and as she squinted at him in the low light of the box Kat saw the ill-curbed amusement.

'Are you having me on, Daniel Bishop? Are you dealing me a pack of lies just to . . . just to——'

'Soften you up? Play on your sympathies?'

'Yes!'

'Have I succeeded?'

'Certainly not! So you fell in love with the wrong woman. Big deal!' She tried to recover badly lost ground.

'At the time, it was,' he said drily.

'Then . . . you mean . . . it was all true?' she faltered.

'Every word.'

'You *weren't* trying to play on my sympathies?'

'Oh, yes, I was doing that . . . but with truth rather than lies.'

'Oh.' She struggled with her conflicting feelings. 'I'm sorry,' she managed grudgingly at last. 'About Elise, I mean.'

'I'm not,' he said with infuriating smoothness. 'I rather enjoyed watching you get hot under the collar on the behalf of my blighted youth . . . although it would be stretching a point to call that scarf a collar, wouldn't it?' His eyes slid from the blossoming scarf to the dipping neckline of the halter-neck dress. Kat took a sudden breath that tightened her breasts against the fabric and became flustered. His eyes slid caressingly down to her glorious red legs, and lingered as she nervously recrossed them.

'Daniel——' she began warningly as he seemed to become lost in his appreciation of her womanly assets.

He shifted in his seat and she flinched almost imperceptibly. He raised a brow along with cool silver eyes. 'No need to be frightened, Kathleen. I don't have anything more to prove tonight.'

The 'more' worried her, and she stiffened. 'I'm not afraid of you.' She tossed her mane proudly. 'If anything, it should be the other way around.'

His eyes narrowed and he smiled faintly to himself. 'Perhaps you're right,' he murmured, and then, to her relief, suddenly started talking about impersonal subjects—the opera, the quality of stage performances he had seen in America and Europe. Impressed by his knowledge, Kat enjoyed the discussion, even when it edged around to her own modest career, and her lack of ambition.

'If everyone was born with your kind of ambition, the world would be crammed with chiefs without indians to order around,' said Kat spiritedly. 'It's not so much a career to me as something that I enjoy doing and can make a living at.'

'Todd said you had received the offer of a regular slot on a satirical television programme.'

'Yes, but it meant commuting to Wellington a couple of days a week and not having the final say over my material. It wasn't worth the hassle just to purvey bubble-gum for the mind.'

He laughed. 'That was a cheap shot—actually, I enjoy that particular programme. I only said that because you denied me my breakfast ration of news.'

'I know.'

He absorbed her smug expression. 'I don't suppose that, in view of my tragic past, you'd care to cry truce on that? I really do need the financial papers to keep up with the daily play at the bank.'

'Uh-uh.' Kat shook her head, unmoved by his plea. 'Not when I've gone to all that trouble of getting up three hours

earlier than usual all week to wade through reams of
capitalistic propaganda. Besides, I think I'm getting the
hang of it now.' She had indeed discovered an instinctive
'feel' for picking a rising share. Daniel, however, was
justifiably sceptical.

'Really?' He asked her a pertinent question regarding a
prominently treated takeover the previous day.

'Oh, yes, I was going to ask you about that. What's
a takeover?' asked Kat innocently, and then burst into
giggles at his snort of smug contempt.

'Are you having me on, Kathleen Kendon?' he asked,
an indulgent smile forming at the back of his eyes as he
mimicked her earlier question.

Catching a flicker of sea-green at the doorway behind
him, Kat was struck by a wicked impulse. She draped
herself suggestively over Daniel's near arm, pressing
her breasts against his warm strength. 'Oh, darling,
I'd love to have you on, any day of the week,' she purred
with sensuous abandon. 'Just say the word, you unbear-
ably sexy man, you, and you can be on me in a trice!'

Her pouting mouth was within kissing distance of
his firm lips, and for a moment she wanted to forget
their audience and taste him again. His smile was still-
born, overtaken by an unmistakable flare of arousal that
drew his features taut. For a moment, she knew, he wanted
that kiss as much as she did.

'What in the hell are you playing at now?' he murmured,
wariness mingled with a faint slur of hunger.

Then Clarissa's cool distaste cleaved between them.
'Really, Kathleen, this pathetic desire of yours for attention
at any cost is very tiresome. I'm afraid you've a lot to learn
about the Bishop men. Daniel has been too often the target
of greedy amorality to be seduced by it, and if you hoped to
make Todd jealous, you've made a mistake there, too. The
poor boy has just dashed away still holding your drink and
looking far more disillusioned than jealous . . .'

CHAPTER SEVEN

'DO Mr Bishop again, Kathleen, it's so *funny*—you really have him off to a T——'

'I'm afraid that this time you'll have to settle for the pale original, Mr Collison.' The chill tones froze the small group of business-suited young men and women. Magically they melted away, leaving the unfortunate Mr Collison stranded beside Kat.

'Mr . . . Mr Bishop——' Before her eyes, the cocky young blood of a few moments ago became a stammering school-boy.

'I trust the fact that you're taking an extended break means that you already have those figures I asked you for half an hour ago?' Daniel asked with a lethally pleasant smile.

'Uh . . . no, not yet, Mr Bishop.' Flushed with discomfort, the young man began to edge towards the doors of the executive suite. 'I . . . goodbye, Kath—Miss Kendon. Uh . . . I'll get on to those figures right away, Mr Bishop.'

'You do that,' said Daniel mildly. As he turned, his voice became curt and imperious. 'Kathleen, I'll see *you* in my office. Now!'

He was on the other side of the room before she found her voice. 'If you'll rephrase that more politely, I might consider it.'

The four secretaries in the plush outer office were suddenly raptly absorbed in their keyboards and VDUs, but there was a collective holding of breath as Daniel turned and slowly, menacingly, retraced his steps. 'It wasn't a request,' he pointed out with liquid calm when he was close enough to impress Kat with his control. 'Security may be even less polite when they throw you off the premises.'

'Afraid you can't handle me all by yourself?' Kat taunted bravely.

'Not can't. Won't. I've already showered once this morning, and to have to do it again would waste valuable time. A man in my position pays other people to soil their hands with the trash.'

It was worth the awed gasps of the secretaries, to whom he was unfailingly polite even in temper, to watch the golden explosion in Kathleen's eyes. Lord, she was beautiful, even in that crumpled rag she no doubt called a dress! The second week of her tenacious occupation of his household had proved even more confounding than the first. Adelaide had changed her tactics and piled on a series of deliberately tedious social engagements but, instead of hanging herself, Kathleen had used the extra rope to tie everyone else into knots. With her sensuous beauty and laid-back charm, she had drifted lazily through the maze, creating interest among the females and excitement among the males. Adelaide was more rattled than Daniel had seen her in years.

He raised an eyebrow at Kathleen's wrath, knowing it would infuriate her even more, and strode briskly into his office. He suspected he knew the reason for her visit . . . at least, he hoped he knew. It would vindicate both his pride and his libido. Perhaps he would no longer have to fight his obsession and, in the process, kill two birds with one stone.

Angrily, Kat stalked after him. It wasn't until he was seated behind his long, low, excessively tidy desk, leaving her hovering in the middle of the thick, grey carpet like a nervous employee, that her temper cooled enough for her to realise that she had been baited into meekly following his order.

'Very clever,' she said cuttingly.

'I thought so,' he agreed smoothly. 'Well, Kathleen? To what do we owe the pleasure of your company, *again?* I would have thought you wasted enough of Todd's time yesterday, insisting that he show you around and entertaining my staff with your antics.'

'If you let Todd out of this ergonomically designed ivory money-tower of yours once in a while, I wouldn't *have* to gatecrash office hours to hold a conversation with the man I'm going to marry,' said Kat, dripping sarcasm as she dropped into the butter-yellow visitor's chair. 'However, as it so happens, I'm here to see you today, not Todd.'

'How delightful,' he said insincerely. 'I can give you five minutes before my next appointment is due.'

'Oh, it shouldn't take that long,' she purred. 'I just came by to warn you of a few bills that will be coming in this month.' She leaned over and plonked a stack of receipts on his pristine blotter. 'Diana rang me this morning and invited me to go shopping for some of my trousseau,' she said cheerfully, relishing the way his brows had snapped together as he saw the first item. He began to leaf, with rising outrage, through the thick pile. 'I hate shopping, but of course you knew that when you made your suggestion to your sister. What were your exact words?' She pondered as if they weren't etched into her brain. 'Oh, yes . . . "the rag-picker's daughter image must go". OK, Daniel, so it's entirely possible that my father *was* actually a ragpicker, but——'

She was cut off by a harsh, guttural explosion.

'Hell! How on earth could you spend this much in one morning?' he roared.' Have you any idea what this lot adds up to?'

'Well, no, not really,' she fluttered, admiring his rage. 'We were having so much fun that I guess we got a little carried away.' That much was true, although she knew to a last cent how much credit she had run up. Revenge apart, Diana Rex had the ability to make even the torture of shopping fun. The affinity she and Kat had felt at their first meeting had continued to grow as Diana declared a firm intention of taking the younger girl under her wing, much to the annoyance of her mother.

'Little! *Little?*' His chair reared back as he shot to his

feet, wrathfully brandishing the evidence of her profligacy
in his clenched fist. 'You call sixteen pairs of Italian shoes a
little carried away? And handbags to match? And *three*
styles of mink? That's not greed, it's obscenity! Why in the
hell didn't Diana stop you——'

'Now, Daniel,' Kat trilled chidingly, 'you can't blame Di.
After all, you told her I could charge what I liked, providing
I deferred to her on matters of taste. You didn't mention
anything about a credit limit——'

'I didn't think I had to!' he thundered, dark blood
suffusing his face. 'You bloodsucking bitch! This is more
than Sharon and Adelaide spend on clothes in six months—
combined. And to think that I actually allowed myself to
think that you——' He bit off the rest of his anger, swinging
around to conceal his livid face as he leant a white-knuckled
fist against the cool glass window.

So Sharon had been right, thought Kat furiously. Todd's
mother had latterly conquered her natural timidity and
revealed a gentle character of surprising resilience. Her
friendship was of necessity more covert than Diana's, but
no less valued. She had bravely included herself into the
morning's shopping expedition, and it was thanks to
Sharon that Kat had realised the true deviousness of
Daniel's motives in suggesting it. Predictably, Kat's
offended pride had reacted badly to Diana's announcement,
at the first salon they had walked into, that she needn't
worry about money since Daniel had given his permission
for everything to go on to the Bishops' unlimited charge
accounts. She had repeated his words verbatim in an effort
to convince Kat that her reticence was unnecessary.

'Daniel *expects* it to cost a fortune. He's a cynic, he even
said he didn't doubt you'd take advantage to the hilt!' Diana
had cried when Kat said she couldn't afford to even
windowshop at the places Diana had on her list to visit. 'If
he expects the worst, who are we to disappoint him? Oh,
Kat, this could be such *fun* if you just let yourself go . . .
Look, have a glass of wine and relax; let Sharon and I do the

hard work and worrying. All you have to do is look beautiful!'

'I don't think Daniel expects the worst at all, not from Kat,' Sharon had stated with her quiet firmness as she sipped her own complimentary glass of wine. 'I think he's coat-trailing. I think he suspects that you have a lot more integrity than you give yourself credit for, Kat.'

'You mean . . . this is some kind of test?' Kat had asked, beginning to figure the angles. She'd taken a fortifying swig of wine which, at nine in the morning, reacted sharply with the lingering traces of toothpaste in her mouth. It had made sense. Would a hardened cynic like Daniel offer someone he believed completely amoral such a tempting opportunity? No, of course not. This was a damned test, and she had nearly passed with flying colours! 'I always hated tests at school.' She'd scowled. 'Even when I *could* pass, I sometimes flunked, on principle.'

'I especially hated the ones that were sprung on you without notice,' Sharon had agreed.

'I used to come out in a rash,' Diana had said. 'Cheers!'

They had all toasted past failures. Slowly Kat had lowered her glass and looked at Sharon. Sharon had looked at Diana and Diana had looked at Kat. Three wicked feminine smiles had emerged simultaneously . . .

Daniel turned from the window and Kat, prepared to enjoy goading him some more, choked on her triumph. He was *smiling*. A horrible, guileless smile that locked her defences on to red alert.

'Have lunch with me?'

'You've *got* to be kidding!' she stuttered furiously. 'After the vile names you just called me? I'd rather eat with a slug.'

The smile widened as he failed to respond to her insult. 'I got the impression that you were rather enjoying my loss of control, but I apologise if that wasn't the case. It just occurred to me that you must be hungry after your orgy of spending. If I know my sister, she wouldn't have paused for anything as mundane as food once she had the bit between her teeth.'

Actually Kat was famished, but admitting it seemed in the nature of a weakness. She should be gorged on the excesses of the morning. 'I can't believe you're asking me just for the pleasure of my company. What happened to your temper tantrum? Or are you planning to put arsenic in the food?'

He slid his hands into his pockets and sauntered around the desk to perch on its edge. He looked down into her beautiful, bewildered and highly suspicious face. Her lips were parted in puzzlement, and it took him a moment to rein in the impulse to part them further with his tongue, to dominate her with his body the way he had failed to do with his mind.

'Is that one of the dresses you bought?'

'Er . . . this?' She looked down at her casual T-shirt dress, its shapelessness conquered by the plaited scarves which served as an attractive belt. While she was stalling, Daniel calmly turned out the label at the nape of her neck and studied the well-known brand name as Kat tried to squirm away.

'Not many women would choose to wear a chainstore dress when they had just bought several thousand dollars' worth of designer fashions. Why bother to go to such absurdly extravagant lengths if you're not going to flaunt the result?'

'I——' Damn! She should have remembered his unerring eye for quality.

'I'll tell you why, Kathleen,' he said silkily. 'Because these bills aren't worth the paper they're written on. You have no intention of wearing any of it. Oh, yes, you came here to gloat, to toss a lighted match into a box of fireworks and enjoy the sight of me making a ranting fool of myself, but then what did you intend doing? Throwing it all back in my face?'

'I have no idea what you're talking about,' she said loftily.

'You mean, you intend keeping everything that you bought?'

'Yes!' she lied triumphantly. Anything to wipe that smug, knowing smile off his face. Damn him for his devious intelligence!

'Oh, well, I suppose there are compensations, even if they're expensive ones,' he said with an aggravating lack of ire. 'At least you've now confessed your greed. Next time I'll remember that you shop like a shark in a feeding frenzy, and take the necessary precautions. And at least I'll no longer have to cringe at introducing you to my friends. I hope you had the sense to take Diana's advice, and you're not merely going to look like a *wealthy* ragpicker's daughter in these new, fine feathers . . .'

'Why, you supercilious creep!' Kat's temper burst the bounds of pretence. She leapt to her feet, determined to salvage some vestige of her victory. 'Laugh this one off: those clothes are right now on their way to the Tremewan Home for Unmarried Mothers, with the suggestion that they be auctioned off to raise money to meet the running costs of the home!'

That did wipe away his smile, but only in favour of an angry admiration. 'When you teach a lesson, you go the whole hog, don't you, Kathleen? I wish I had a few people with your ruthlessness on my board of directors. How does smoked salmon and avocado sound for lunch? Chilled soup and fresh rolls with flaky crusts glazed with milk? Raspberries and cream? And champagne to celebrate our generous donation to charity?'

Kat's mouth was watering so much, she was afraid that if she spoke she would drool. She closed her eyes against the seduction of her senses, but the velvety darkness against her lids conspired against her.

'Such raspberries, Kathleen—sunwarmed, fat and ripe and red, bursting sweet and tart upon the tongue . . .' Intent on luring her into his net, he lured himself. Her sensuous expression triggered other memories . . . her whipped cream breasts and their raspberry crests. His hunger was suddenly sharp, and he summoned his full powers of persuasion. 'It's past time, isn't it, that we dropped this absurd game?'

'Game?' Her eyes snapped open, still slightly glazed.

'Of one-upmanship,' he said. 'Believe it or not, I do have Todd's interests at heart. Perhaps if we got to know each other a little better, we might be able to find some common ground for compromise . . .' He lied through his teeth. He had learned his lesson from Elise. He was not a man who could live with compromise, he enjoyed winning too much. While Elise had walked away from their affair with her pride intact, he had suffered the humiliation of knowing that he had been prepared to sacrifice both principles and pride for an illusion that he himself had fostered. From that day on he had controlled his imagination rather than vice versa, channelling it into more productive pursuits.

'I . . . I was going to see if Todd and I could go to lunch together . . .' Kat began, sinfully tempted by his reasonableness.

'He can't take you, he's not even here, he's at a board meeting,' said Daniel, not making the mistake of sounding inordinately pleased about it. He reached for the intercom on his desk and pressed the button. 'Miss Coulter, could you please ask Mr Bateman to re-schedule our appointment for three. And get Miss Paine on the line for me.'

It was only a few seconds later that the yellow phone on his desk rang with a soft burr. He picked it up, not taking his eyes off Kathleen, who remained frozen in indecision.

'Clarissa? I'll have to cancel lunch. Mmm? No, I haven't forgotten—this evening at eight. I'll see you then.'

Very cool and calm. He might have been postponing a dental appointment. Kat was fascinated. 'Didn't she even ask why?'

'She trusts me.'

'You mean she doesn't care,' retorted Kat, chilled by this confirmation of the extent of 'understanding' between the affianced pair. No wonder Todd despaired. She found it difficult to comprehend, though, how the tempestuous man from the library could be satisfied with such a pallid arrangement. OK, so he had turned his back on love, but what about passion? You didn't generate that out of the kind of nothingness that existed between Daniel and Clarissa . . . unless they had agreed that each would seek other outlets. Kat went hot and cold at such bloodless premeditation, her unwilling curiosity driving her to say, 'OK, I'll come to lunch, but only if you take me to the most expensive place in town.' And if things got too far out of hand she could always subvert his sudden conviction in her personal integrity by picking a fight and staging a vulgar scene.

'I can't promise it's the most expensive, but it *is* the most exclusive,' he murmured. 'Would you mind waiting in the outer office while I make a call? I shan't be long . . .'

The most exclusive place in town turned out to be five storeys up—the penthouse apartment. Protest would have been hypocritical; Kat had been dying to poke her nose into his private retreat, and it hadn't been on the agenda of the previous day's tour. Would it possess the starkly impersonal modernity of the Rex, Bishop offices, or the museum-like antique order of his family home?

It was neither. The apartment was a comfortable mixture of styles, decorated in warm, autumnal shades, sensuous and relaxing.

'I like it,' said Kat with some surprise, slowly touring the large, square living area with its spectacular view of the city from the large grassed patio outside the sliding glass doors.

'Thank you,' said Daniel simply, shedding his jacket and unbuttoning his waistcoat. He watched her move around his sanctuary with her long-limbed, lazy grace, admiring his possessions with tactile curiosity.

'I kind of expected a showcase bachelor pad, calculated to impress,' she confessed as she touched the patinated smoothness of a kauri rocking-chair.

'I don't entertain here. I come here to unwind, or when

I'm working overnight on confidential documents that can't leave the building.' He stretched to relieve limbs that had been cramped at his desk all morning. As he did so, he noticed her covert study of the muscular contractions taking place beneath his crisp, white cotton shirt. She nibbled her lower lip, her big golden eyes lowering . . .

He turned away to hide the jolt of knowledge, the silken certainty that sank to his loins. She wanted him. Regardless of anything else, he fascinated her quite as much as she did him. He would be able to use that. He would take her away from his nephew for the simple reason that he wanted her himself. Oh, there were other, more complex reasons involved, but this one overshadowed the rest.

'Would you like a drink?' he asked, over his shoulder. 'No? Then I'll just go and tell Mrs Chatterton we're here. I rang ahead to warn her there would be two of us. Make yourself at home. The bathroom's through on the left if you need it.'

Kat didn't need to make herself at home. She already felt completely at ease with her surroundings. She slipped off her multi-coloured sandals—doubtless Daniel had noticed that they were no more exclusive than her dress—and walked across the thick carpet to look out at the rooftop oasis of greenery. Full-sized trees in huge tubs shaded one side of the patio, preserving the privacy that a tall building nearby threatened. There were ceramic pots of flowers and shrubs, and a tiled area where a small fountain played beside a grouping of white tubular garden furniture.

'Contemplating running barefoot through my grass?' Daniel had returned, carrying an ice-bucket containing a foil-topped bottle and two tulip glasses.

'Is it real?'

'Of course.' Daniel opened the champagne and poured her a glass. 'I never settle for anything less than the real thing.'

Except where marriage is concerned, Kat wanted to say, but she was loath to disturb the fragile truce, so instead she slid open the door and went out. The grass felt like cool velvet under her overheated feet.

Daniel leant against the open door, sipping his champagne. In the simple cotton dress she suddenly looked like a girl masquerading as a woman—clean-skinned, sparkling-eyed, eager for experience. Daniel felt a momentary impulse to protect her from his dishonourable intentions, but shrugged it off with impatience. She had already proved that she could well look after herself.

'Do you think . . . can we eat out here?' She indicated the table by the fountain, shaded by a large white umbrella.

'I don't see why not.'

It was a long, leisurely lunch, every bit as good as Daniel had promised. And the company was even better. Kat had dined with an indolent, likeable stranger who had teased and flirted and fascinated and made her laugh. A quixotic Daniel who had drawn her into a charmed world, not once pricking her with the devastating sarcasm of which he was capable. They stayed away from dangerous subjects, and Kat amused him with an exhaustingly funny description of her morning's encounter with the alien world of *haute couture*. She so enjoyed the novelty of his indulgence that she didn't notice his eyes narrow when she mentioned that Sharon, too, had accompanied her on the wicked spree.

'In fact, she was worse than Diana. She was all for getting jewellery, too, but I had to draw the line somewhere. Do you think they have a grudge against you, Daniel!' She grinned at him. 'They were awfully keen to waste your money for you.'

'You really are a charmer, aren't you?' Daniel murmured drily. 'I suppose the next time I turn around, I'll find Adelaide in your corner, too.'

Kat gurgled a laugh. 'I don't think there's any fear of that.'

'Mmm, you never even bother to *try* with my mother, do you? And yet in an odd way I think she respects you for not caring a fig for her opinion. Also for your insistence on working, when you know very well that Todd would be happy to indulge your every whim.'

That was going *too* far. 'Then how come she kicked up such a terrible fuss about it?' Working for Gino kept her in touch with reality beyond the velvet-lined cocoon of wealth she had been inhabiting lately, as well as boosting her finances which, although relieved by not having to pay living expenses, had to sustain her until her next theatrical engagement, a walk-on a few weeks hence. She and Todd had had a torrid row about her standing in for one of Gino's night-shift waitresses who was sick. Todd had whined that it would ruin her image as a beautiful parasite, but Kat had put her foot down. Gino needed her, the temporary help he had hired in the past had usually been poorly trained and often dishonest, and an old friendship deserved more loyalty than a new. Kat was going to help him and that was that.

'I think it was the way you announced it that caused the fuss,' said Daniel drily. It had been at one of Adelaide's formal dinners. It had started late and it was nearly eleven before dessert was served. Kat had hurried through hers and then leapt up with the excuse that she had to be at work in an hour. To the delicious shock of those present, she had explained that she was a waitress in an all-night restaurant, 'although I do dishes, too'. Everyone had automatically looked towards Adelaide, who had gone a mottled shade of pink and announced that Kat was 'having one of her little jokes at our expense'. Twenty minutes later Kat had proved it was no joke by popping in to say goodnight in her 'uniform'—a black vinyl mini skirt, black stockings and a white singlet top that showed off her spectacular figure. Adelaide was still fighting a rearguard action, furious that her friends should think that a house-guest, near family to boot—should be known to be 'skivvying' for a living.

'Yes, well, she had to know some time, didn't she?' said Kat unrepentantly. At least it had quietened Todd. As long as Adelaide was outraged, he was happy. Daniel, too, had

had a few choice words to say the next time they had encountered each other: not, to her surprise, about the job so much as her insistence that it would make no difference to her ability to fulfil all the daytime social obligations that Adelaide was heaping upon her. He had also been scathing about her 'uniform', and told her he thought Todd was mad to allow her to run around the streets at night, dressed like a prostitute. Kat had been equally scathing about his snobbery, and not for the world would she admit that the snatched hours of broken sleep *were* beginning to get her down and she was getting more than her fair share of amorous customers in the restaurant. Gino's son, a big, brawny lad, was a fine deterrent, and Gino himself took issue with those who hassled his waitresses, but they weren't always to hand.

'You're not working just for the sake of it, are you, Katheleen? Just to make one of your blasted points? There's no need—surely your friend can find someone else,' said Daniel abruptly. 'You should have spent this morning in bed rather than waltzing around the shops.'

Kat's mouth opened to snap a reply, then she laughed. 'It was your idea,' she pointed out, and he frowned as his eyes slid over the white dress.

'You've lost some weight.' It was almost an accusation.

'I needed to shed a few pounds.'

'I don't like you working there.'

She meant his gaze calmly. 'Tough.'

'I suppose if I *ordered* you to stay on there, you'd quit,' he growled.

'I should hope I'm not that predictable.' She grinned.

'Oh, rest assured, you're not.'

Seeing the humorous light re-enter his eyes, Kat decided that it was time to focus the spotlight on him for a change. She asked him the time, and then took the opportunity to question him about the exquisite old-fashioned gold fob-watch he wore. That he recognised the ploy was obvious, but it seemed that he was prepared to indulge her, and soon he was diverted by his own interest. He showed her his workroom, an extension of the one at the house where no one dared set foot in his absence. He even did his own cleaning there, the maid told Kat.

She was secretly enchanted at the change that came over Daniel as he pointed out some of the more important pieces in his collection of clocks and watches, and explained some of the disassembled mechanisms he was repairing. His initial diffidence crumbled into almost boyish eagerness when he realised her questions were prompted by genuine interest rather than politeness. Obviously few people bothered to display more than a cursory interest in what was a very esoteric hobby. She was touched by the tender realisation that Daniel wasn't the model of self-sufficiency he first appeared. He needed someone to share his enthusiasm, his sense of wonder in the beautiful objects he had assembled. He needed someone like Kat to trigger his emotions! Ironically, they were so engrossed in their subject that they lost track of time, and Daniel was almost flustered when he had to rush away to his postponed appointment. But even then the fragile pleasure of the afternoon was not lost for, going down in the express lift, Daniel kissed her. It was not a stormy kiss, full of aggressive passion, nor yet one of mere friendliness, but somewhere in between, warm and slow, tilting her heart with its hint of promise. It was a kiss of peace, a kiss of exploration, a kiss of . . . expectation!

CHAPTER EIGHT

'KAT? Hey, Katalina, wake up in there! Table four are still waiting for their iced water. Say . . . are you OK?'

'Huh?' Kat blinked at the fingers snapping in front of her face. Angie, Gino's teenage daughter, was looking at her with concern as the sights, sounds and smells of the restaurant whirled back into focus. 'Oh . . . sure . . . just tired, I suppose.'

It wasn't a lie, just a gross understatement. Kat was shattered! So much for her foolish expectations following that dreamy lunch. The next time Kat had seen Daniel, he had been Mr Hyde again, spitting venomous fury. Thank heavens Freya had offered her a bolt-hole at her friend's flat. All Kat wanted to do when this shift was over was curl up into a ball and try and sleep away her troubles. She hadn't slept a wink in the past twenty-four hours, and everything suddenly seemed too much . . .

She had returned from work the previous morning, later than usual—half-past five—and was distinctly shaky when Seth let her into the kitchen. Softened by the gift for his nephew of a soggy kitten that Kat had rescued from the pool and kept in her room until Sharon had apologetically mentioned Adelaide's animal-fur allergy—which didn't seem to extend to dead-animal-fur, like mink—Seth had made it his job to turn off the alarms and be up to let her in and provide a soporific cup of chocolate milk to take up to bed.

This morning he was shocked when he opened the door and she nearly fell across the threshold.

'Kathleen, what happened?'

'You really don't want to know,' said Kat wearily, one hand held protectively over the torn strap of her white

126

singlet. Now she was home, she just wanted to forget the whole sordid incident.

'But . . . are you hurt? Kat, you're shaking!'

'Pure rage.' She grinned weakly at him, his concern soothing the queasiness that had knotted her stomach. 'I'm not hurt, Seth, really, just a bit shaken. There was this man . . .' She swallowed, shuddering slightly as she remembered.

'Man?' Seth bristled protectively. Kat had discovered that the ex-fighter had very chivalrous instincts where women were concerned.

'What man?' The harsh demand came from the other side of the room. Kat looked across at the man in the doorway. He wore an expensive black robe that covered him from neck to knee, and an expression of such savagely reined-in aggression that she immediately felt queasy again.

'Daniel! I . . . what are you doing up?'

'I have an early breakfast meeting.' He put the empty coffee-cup in his hand down on the marble bench, not taking his eyes off Kat. 'What man?'

'I . . .' Kat licked her lips. Heavens, she was going to sound like a fool, and Daniel was sure to rub it in. She made a helpless gesture with her free hand, and that drew his gaze to the other, clamped over the tear in her top. Fire flickered through thin blue ice.

'Did he do that?'

'He got a bit carried away,' Kat said nervously, wondering why she was making excuses for the lecherous wretch. But she knew why. Looking into Daniel's eyes, she realised the origin of the term looking 'blue murder'. He was drunk, Daniel, he just didn't know what he was doing. I could handle it.'

'Oh, yes, it looks like it,' he bit off with searing contempt, padding closer. Kat wished that she hadn't slipped her shoes off her aching feet the minute she had staggered in the door. Even in his bare feet Daniel topped her by what suddenly felt like a mile. 'Who was it, Kathleen? A customer?'

Kat nodded. Eyes locked, neither of them noticed Seth edging discreetly out of the room. If ever there were two people who didn't need interference, it was these two . . .

'And where in the hell was that Italian friend of yours while one of his customers were mauling you?' he asked savagely.

'I . . . it wasn't in the restaurant.'

'In the *street?* He did this to you in the street?' Daniel swore, one hand coming up to cup her bruised shoulder. 'Who was he, Kathleen?'

'I don't know. He's not a regular, if that's what you mean,' said Kathleen, trying to ignore the way his fingers were moving against her skin. 'Anyway, it didn't happen in the street. We were in a taxi . . .' She winced as the caressing fingers suddenly dug into her skin. The incredulous silence stretched . . .

'In a *taxi?* You were in a taxi with him? A drunken man you didn't even *know?*' His hand dropped as if her skin burnt him, but his voice was icy with disbelief.

Put that way, it sounded indefensible. 'Yes, but——'

'Where were you going? Back to his place?'

'*No!* Of course not.'

'There's no of course about it. You pick up a customer, a drunk, cosy up to him in a taxi dressed like *that!* What in the hell did you *expect* him to do?'

'It wasn't like that!' she flared. After the tentative understanding of the day before, his contempt came as a rude shock. This was what he *really* thought of her. In his anger, the depth of his mistrust was fully revealed. Kat felt a deep thrust of pain which she swiftly converted to angry pride. 'He got into the taxi that Gino called for me. He seemed quite decent at first, suggesting we split the fare. For goodness' sake——' her outrage inflamed further '—you can't believe that I *invited* him——'

'The way you're dressed is an open invitation,' Daniel ground out. 'Why on earth don't you wear a coat? Or change into something less blatantly provocative before you go out in the street at night?'

'It was hot and I was tired,' said Kat sullenly, knowing that he had a valid point. 'And I'm even more tired now, standing here having to listen to your self-righteous lecturing.' Drawing herself up to her full height, she stepped around him. But she should have known that he wouldn't let her have the last word.

'Damn you, Kathleen, don't you turn your back on me.' He hauled her round by her free arm. 'I haven't finished yet.' His darkly shadowed jaw was dangerously brittle with tension, his lean body suddenly bulky with threat. 'I knew this was going to happen. I *knew* you wouldn't be able to keep out of trouble.'

'Oh, omniscient now, are we?' Kat mocked tightly. 'My, you sound almost *pleased*.'

'Well, it's not going to happen again. You're not going back there.' He *was* pleased. His voice was grim with triumph.

'The hell I'm not!' Kat sparked furiously, trying to rid herself of his iron grip on her wrist. 'I'll work where and when I damned well please!'

'Not while you're living under *my* roof, you won't,' said Daniel grimly. 'And if you defy me, I'll have your Italian friend's restaurant shut down by the health department.'

'You wouldn't.'

'Try me.' The invitation was thick with menace. 'I have a great deal of influence in this city, Kathleen. If necessary, I'll use it.'

And this was the man that she had been afraid she was falling in love with . . . this icicle! This ruthless dictator!

'You hypocrite!' she shouted at him, afraid that if she didn't scream she'd burst into foolish tears. 'It's all right for *you* to maul me, isn't it? I don't hear you ordering me to stay away from the bank in case some lecherous pig tries to rape me in the lift! And you didn't even have the excuse of being *drunk*!'

His grip tightened at her defiant sneer, and Kat struggled against him with fresh outrage. Her stockinged feet suddenly slipped on the tiled floor, and she grabbed at his chest to regain her balance. His arm snapped around her waist and he spread his feet to take the blow of her body without staggering. Her thigh slid inadvertently between his legs, parting his robe, brushing against his nudity. They both froze. The muscle of his manhood stirred and Kat drew a very shaky breath. His eyes registered anger at his body's betrayal. Surely he would now thrust her from him in disgust? But he didn't, he continued to hold her against his growing arousal.

'Let me go,' Kat whispered, ashamed herself of the hot need that didn't care about his contempt as long as he filled the emptiness that ached inside her.

'Why should I?' he muttered thickly, putting his mouth to the side of her throat. 'I'm not the hypocrite, you are. And you're a damned tease into the bargain. It wouldn't be rape if I took you, Kathleen, and you know it.'

Her head fell back. 'Daniel, no . . .' she said weakly, as he rubbed his powerful body against her. Weariness, anger and her shocked disillusionment at his insults melted away with her resistance. Why deny it? This was what she wanted . . . had wanted all her life . . . this feeling of *belonging* to someone. Beyond scruple, she wanted him. Other people didn't matter. The fact that he belonged to another woman didn't matter. For now, he was hers.

She arched against him, trembling, and his groan was muffled against her skin as his hands moved druggingly over her.

'Daniel, yes . . .' he corrected her in a rasping whisper, moving his lips against her bare shoulder where the torn strap had fallen away. He tugged at the stretchy fabric, pulling the damaged edge down over her white cotton bra. Her nipple was a dark point against the thin white cotton. He found it with his teeth as he cupped his hand around her lush fullness, his thighs tightening around her trapped leg, forcing her hips into intimate contact with his potent maleness. Kat's fingers dug into the taut muscles ridging his waist as he roughly pulled aside her bra and began to suckle the creamy flesh beneath. She was so far gone that she was pulling at the loose tie to his robe when there was a muffled thud in the hallway.

Daniel dropped her like a hot coal. They stared at each other with a horrified awe that was every bit as mutual as the incandescent passion of a moment before. Daniel's face was taut and pale, with streaks of red across his cheekbones as he rewrapped his robe. Kat forced her numb fingers to straighten her bra and T-shirt, flushing wildly at the savage look in his eyes.

'What's going on down here? Did I hear shouting just now?' Todd, bleary-eyed and disgruntled, shoved through the kitchen door. He stopped, not too sleepy-headed to miss the tension electrifying the atmosphere. 'Kat? Daniel? What's going on?'

For a heartbeat Daniel hesitated, and Kat thought that it was going to be all right, that their shared passion had obliterated the ugly allegations that had preceded it. She smiled tentatively at him, but for some reason her silent offer of peace seemed to trigger a violent recoil.

'Look at her. What in the hell do you *think* has been going on?' he snarled at his startled nephew. 'Your fiancée seems to have trouble distinguishing one man from another. I'm the second tonight who's had the pleasure of handling the merchandise.'

His exit was an agony of triumph. Todd's eyes rounded on Kat's face. Tears? Oh, no, his champion was crying. What had he done? What had *they* done?

'Kat . . . Kathleen . . . did he . . .? Are you hurt?'

'No. Yes . . . no.' Kat closed her eyes, futility shattering the brittle shell of her heart. She loved him. She had thought that she had got to know him a little—that he had come to respect her, but it was all sham. He thought she was little better than a whore. It was no longer funny, a careless game. It *mattered,* more than she had ever dreamed anyone's opinion could. 'I want out, Todd. Now. Tonight. No negotiating, no delays. I want to leave, Anna or no Anna!'

That was when Todd had thrown himself on her mercy. Guiltily, remorsefully, he had confessed: there *was* no Anna, no young and tender lover. He had made her up, made it all up, because he had needed Kat.

The fictitious Anna had merely been bait to lure Kat's unwitting co-operation in a matchmaking conspiracy—or rather, match-*breaking* conspiracy. Kat had been set among the pigeons to challenge their complacent view of the future. Her sultry beauty was to divert Daniel's attention from the incomparable Clarissa long enough to allow him to see the error of his ways. Her characterisation, with all its attendant inconsistencies, was supposed to infuriate and tantalise him, her frank unconventionality to challenge his own commitment to convention, her humour and wit to intrigue him, her warmth to pierce his cynicism, her strength of will and purpose to impress. In short, Kat was a living example of all that Daniel planned to deny himself by marrying with a cold heart.

If the conspiracy came as a shock to Kat, the identity of Todd's co-conspirators was even more devastating.

Sharon . . . quiet, demure, shy-eyed Sharon Bishop had been the mastermind, and her first lieutenant was the irrepressible Diana. Like the Three Musketeers they had swashbuckled to the rescue of the Bishop Dynasty when they saw it threatened by a loveless liaison.

Understanding their motivation didn't lessen Kat's feelings of bitter anger and hurt betrayal. She had closed her ears to Todd's pleading and decided then and there to pack and leave. She was in the pink bedroom, scrabbling in the closet, when Todd had hurriedly wheeled in the big gun and left. Sharon, still in her nightgown and négligé, had been eloquent, with a sixth sense of Kat's weak spots.

'You have every right to feel the way you do, Kathleen,

and I wouldn't blame you if you chose to walk out and never speak to any of us ever again. But I hope you won't. I hope that, whatever happens, we can continue the friendship that we have begun.'

'Friends don't lie to each other.'

'I know. I'm sorry. But, Kathleen, none of us really expected this hare-brained plan to actually *work*. And when it did I suppose we got carried away by its momentum. Todd had met you a few times and told us how much fun you were and how he wished Daniel would marry someone warm and generous like you instead of that emotionally tight-fisted paragon of his. I said "what if . . ." and it sort of all grew from there.

'I admit that our motives weren't entirely altruistic. Diana thought her mother needed to be saved from her own calcifying narrow-mindedness. Todd wanted to be taken more seriously as a mature adult with opinions of his own that needed to be listened to, if not actually acted on, and I was getting rather tired of being taken for granted. Clarissa treats me just as Adelaide does, as if I'm a living monument to family history. I'm not. I'm a woman with feelings and emotions and a future that doesn't automatically have to include everything Bishop. It was wrong of us to use you as a catalyst for our problems, but as I see it you weren't *totally* averse to getting involved with us, once you got to know Daniel.

'Primarily it *has* been for Daniel, I promise you that. A conspiracy of love, you might call it, because Daniel deserves so much more than he allows himself to expect. He came home from Europe when his father was dying, quite eager to settle down in every sense of the word . . . poised to fully enjoy the rest of his life.' Sharon sighed. 'Only the woman he wanted to settle down with didn't share his respect for roots.'

'Elise . . .' Kat murmured. Sharon paused in her persuasive task.

'Yes . . . how did you know?'

'Daniel told me.'

'*Daniel* did? Goodness! I thought he never talked . . .' Sharon trailed off, tact winning over curiosity. 'Anyway, intellectually Daniel found all the challenges he needed developing Rex, Bishop, but as far as his private life goes . . . for the past ten years he's become increasingly cautious. His eligibility has made him a prime target for ambitious women, and I think he found the constant pursuit rather wearisome. In a sense, I think Clarissa is a defence—not that he would ever admit it. But Daniel has a very deep-seated desire for a family of his own, and he's not about to give that away just because love proved such a failure. *Now* he feels he had a lucky escape, but the hindsight only emphasises what he sees as an appalling lack of judgement where Elise was concerned. In ten years he's never even come close to falling in love again. *He* thinks it's because he's too cynical and experienced to ever find his ideal woman, but I fervently believe, Kathleen, that this fabulous *ideal* of his—based as it is on standards of reason and intellect rather than emotion—is to blame. Because he refuses to make the same mistake twice, he's actively avoided the very type of woman who *could* inspire him to love: a woman he can't command at the snap of his fingers, a woman to rattle him, to *demand* his love, to impel him to step out of his sophisticated shell. I'm sure the reason that he hasn't found someone "suitable" until now is because something inside of him *knows* that marriage without love won't satisfy him half as much as he has convinced himself it will. This time, though, Adelaide's manoeuvrings and his own desire to make a decision and get on with producing a family happened to coincide.'

Sharon drew a deep breath, slowing down as she registered Kat's unwilling fascination. 'Kat, this workable substitute for love which he has devised is going to turn into a prison that his own sense of family honour is going to make it impossible to escape from. He needs a woman by his side who has human flaws and failings, who will appeal to the tenderness in him, not just the strength, who will engage his passion, not just his protection. He and Clarissa are like two diamonds, impervious to each other, brilliant but cold, with all their fire trapped inside. If we love him, Kat, can we just walk away, knowing what we're allowing him to condemn himself to?'

'I don't . . .' Kat couldn't quite voice the lie. Besides, Sharon *knew* . . . knew what Kat herself had only just discovered.

'He feels something for you, Kat. Isn't it worth finding out what? Isn't he worth taking a few risks for? Can you walk away——'

'It's not a matter of walking away,' said Kat in despair. 'You can't manipulate people into loving . . .'

'No, but you can put them into situations where they can discover the possibilities for themselves. There was never any question that in the end Daniel will marry exactly who he chooses to marry, but maybe he's not aware of all the choices. "Some cupid kills with arrows, some with traps", Kat.'

Kat sighed wearily as she bumped open the door to the restaurant with a practised swat of her hip and carried her tray out to table four. She was almost there when she saw the man talking to Federico, Gino's son. She began to tremble, and to her horror the tray tilted wildly in her hands, the frosted ice-water jug and glasses smashing to the tiled floor, splattering nearby diners with their contents.

'I'm terribly sorry . . .' Kat stammered, staring unseeingly at the mess. She knelt to clumsily pick up some of the shattered glass. Everything seemed to be happening in slow motion, a roaring in her ears blocking out the confusion around her. She looked at her hand in dumb surprise as blood suddenly began to well out of her thumb. A large, snowy white handkerchief wrapped itself around the injury, and then Kat felt herself being picked up and set on her feet, a firm arm anchored around her waist. Gino came bustling out of the kitchen and Kat could see his mouth opening and shutting, but she couldn't hear what he was saying for the roaring in her ears.

'Kathleen?' The smoky inflection penetrated her numbness as she realised that it was Daniel who was holding her, bracing her with the warm security of his chest as it appeared her knees were too weak to hold her.

'Why didn't you tell me, Katalina?' Gino reproved her. 'Of course you shouldn't be working.' His volatile expression darkened, his big hand making a fist in front of his face. 'If that man shows his face here again, Federico and I will deal with him. No one messes *my* girls. You go home. We can manage . . . Mama can do the tables. You take her, Mr Bishop——'

'I intend to.'

Kat jerked around against the restraining arm. The ruthless determination in the brief words was echoed in the predatory flicker of silver in his eyes. Kat stiffened, disgusted by her own weakness.

'I'm not going anywhere with you!' she hissed at him. 'Leave me alone.'

'Impossible, I'm afraid,' he said gravely, not taking his eyes off her flushed face, noting her glazed tiredness and the slight betraying puffiness around her eyes. 'You're in no state to work. Come on, I'm taking you home.'

'Home?' Where was home? *Where the heart is,* whispered her romantic soul, and she blinked against a resurgence of weak tears. She had never cried over a man before, but she had more than made up for it in the last twenty-four hours. She wasn't going to let *him* have the satisfaction of knowing how vulnerable she was, though. And she had no intention of going anywhere with a man who thought she was beneath contempt. Why was he here, anyway? To get her fired? To carry out his threat to close Gino down? The thought made her panic.

'No, Gino, I can't go with him,' she said wildly, waving her bandaged hand. 'You don't know what he's going to do. He's going to plant cockroaches or rats or something . . .'

'Totally disorientated,' said Daniel smoothly, and to
Kat's bewilderment Gino nodded paternally. Couldn't he
see? She felt herself sway with weak rage.

In a few very confused minutes, Daniel used his sophisticated charm and a smoothly solicitous manner to best
effect. Kat found herself bundled into the Mercedes which
was double-parked outside the restaurant, and Gino's
admonitions not to worry about work until she had got over
her shock were still ringing in her ears.

'How dare you?' Kat struggled fruitlessly to defeat the
central locking system as Daniel nudged her across into the
passenger seat. 'This is kidnapping. There's nothing *wrong*
with me. Oh, why didn't Gino *listen* . . .'

'Because you were raving and because he could see for
himself that there *is* something wrong. You're overtired and
overwrought. Freya told me that you hadn't had any sleep,
and by the look of you you haven't eaten either. You're in
delayed shock. I couldn't believe it when she told me that
you'd gone off to work.'

'You spoke to Freya?'

'She rang the house. She was rather concerned about you.
She said you insisted on going to work as usual, even
though you hardly knew what you were doing. She also had
a few choice insults for me.' His voice, implacably gentle
and soothing, softened further. 'I'm sorry if I hurt you,
Kathleen. I didn't intend to lose my temper, it just
happened. You seemed to take being attacked so casually.
Of course, I realise now that I handled it all wrong, that it
wasn't casualness but shock. I take back every vile word I
said. Getting into the taxi was a stupid move, but I don't
think you'll ever do it again. I only wish I'd been there to
see the driver deck him.' His voice was no longer soft, but
grim with satisfaction.

'H-how did you know that?' As soon as the taxi driver had
realised what was happening in the back seat, he had
stopped the car, hauled out the offender and delivered him
the rough justice of his fist. 'I've got a daughter your age,'

he had told the much relieved and embarrassed Kat.

'I rang the company this morning to see if I could trace the bastard who hurt you. He can consider himself lucky that your driver didn't check him for ID—and Gino says he paid cash at the restaurant, so there's no joy in finding him that way.' He caught Kat's stifled sound of shock and controlled the brief revival of his anger. 'Sorry, kitten, it's just frustration. I'm not going to take it out on you again. But we're certainly going to have to re-think your work habits.'

Kat stiffened. 'If you think you can blackmail me into giving up——'

'Not blackmail—compromise.'

'I thought they were synonyms in your language,' she sniped, hardly believing what she was hearing. First he apologised, now he was actually bowing to her determination! And the way he called her kitten was sending shivers down her tired spine.

There was a self-derisive humour in his reply. 'I didn't say I *liked* it. However, I have to respect your loyalty to your friends. If you *must* work at Gino's, there'll be no more taxis. Seth will chauffeur you.'

'A waitress—taking a chauffeured limousine to work? It's absurd!' said Kat shakily, grappling with the knowledge that he actually *cared*! The apology had been unaccustomed but genuine.

'Mmm, I rather thought it would appeal to your well-developed sense of the ridiculous.' Daniel deftly twisted her meaning to his advantage.

It did, rather, but Kat refused to share his smile. 'I won't——'

'Be very careful what you say next, Kathleen,' he warned her pleasantly. 'A compromise demands *mutual* concessions. Why take a risk if you don't have to? You won't impress anyone by being stubborn about this . . . particularly as there won't *be* a restaurant for you to work in if you won't stoop to compromise your lofty pride.'

'And you don't impress *me* with empty threats,' said Kat stoutly. He wouldn't close Gino down, she knew that now. He had merely been trying to shake her into acknowledging her own foolishness.

'But you'll take up the offer of the lift, anyway?' prompted Daniel gently, perceiving the trust inherent in the casual contempt of her reply, and amused by his own chest-puffing response to such disarming naïveté. Of course, her trust was a defence in itself—how could he bring himself to betray such innocence?

'Maybe,' Kat temporised, knowing full well she would. 'Hey, where are we going?' She had suddenly noticed their direction. 'I'm not going back to that expensive mausoleum of yours. I'm staying with Freya—she's expecting me.'

'Not any more,' he countered smoothly. 'We're going to the apartment, as it happens, for a little chat. I think it's time that you cleared up one or two mysteries for me. And don't give me that innocent look; you know what I'm talking about.' His eyes gleamed in the dark interior of the car. 'I shouldn't think you'll hold out very long. Sleep deprivation is a very effective interrogation tool . . .'

'You make me sound like a terrorist spy,' said Kat faintly. Sharon's comments suddenly seemed awfully naïve. Daniel would never forgive her interference, however unwitting, in his life.

'You're certainly showing a fairly lethal commitment to destroying *my* peace of mind,' he said with unnerving accuracy. 'Now shut up and let me concentrate on my driving. You're distraction enough, just sitting there within reach.'

The hum of the car, the gentle caress of the air-conditioning and the soft music from the quadrophonic tape deck took its toll, and Kat's eyelids began to droop, fluttering panic easing at the fatalistic acceptance that she could do nothing to prevent the reckoning at hand. In a way, it was rather a relief . . .

Walking into the lift with the sleeping woman draped in his arms, Daniel nodded in amusement at the security guard whose expression was a mixture of shock and curiosity. He shifted Kat's weight against his chest as he keyed the penthouse lift, looking down at the lovely face tipped back across the crook of his elbow as the doors closed. Her sensuous mouth was parted slightly, the rounded swell of her full breasts stretching the white fabric of her flimsy top as they rose and fell in slow rhythm. She was tall and no lightweight, but he enjoyed the effort it required to hold her. In all ways, it would take a strong man to hold her.

The lift opened directly into the apartment and he strode with her into the bedroom, the fragrance and feel of her body against him teasing at his aroused senses. The jealousy and possessiveness he was discovering in himself with regard to Kathleen was unnerving. He needed time to come to terms with it.

He tucked her to his side as he pulled back the pale gold quilt and placed her gently on the cream fitted undersheet. Framed in the smooth silk, the honey of her skin took on a fresh lustre. She looked at home there, in his bed.

Under the light tan, her face was pale with exhaustion. Gently he stroked a few stray strands of red-gold from her cheek. If she was going to sleep comfortably, and she needed to sleep, she should be freed from those constricting clothes. He hesitated, his sensual mouth curving cynically. That wasn't it at all. He wanted to savour the sight of her nude in his bed, her lovely body soft and relaxed and trusting, a deliciously erotic challenge to his resolute self-control . . .

When Kat opened her eyes, it was only just light. Through the vertical cream blinds she could see that the sky outside the long bank of windows was navy, tinged with pink and gold. Dawn? Dawn in a strange bed . . . a bed that was warm and male-scented? Kat let out a thick groan as she remembered. She sat up abruptly and discovered the state of her undress as the slippery silk sheet slid to her waist.

Her gasp was echoed by a faint sound from the door. She snatched up the sheet and held it protectively in front of her, blinking heavy-eyed at the man silhouetted by the light from the hallway behind him.

'Daniel!' And then, because she really wasn't *sure,* 'What have you *done?*'

He clicked a switch at his elbow and soft lights above the wide bed sprang into prominence, bathing Kat in a golden glow.

'*We* haven't done anything . . . yet.' He sauntered towards her, relaxed in his white cotton sweater and dark trousers. 'Your virtue, such as it is, is still intact,' he told her with the shadow of a smile. 'How do you feel?' He checked her thumb, now painlessly taped.

'What have you done with my clothes?' she demanded as he sat on the bed. He smiled and her well-rested temper sizzled. 'Damn you, I want——'

'Let's skip the outraged virgin bit, shall we, Kathleen?' he said silkily. 'Business before . . . we discuss what we both want . . .'

'Business?' squeaked Kat, playing for time. Her eyes slid past him to rest gratefully on the bedside carriage clock. 'Goodness, look at the time! I thought it was earlier, it's so dark outside. Eight o'clock. Shouldn't you be getting ready for work?'

His smile grew tigerish. He leaned forward, placing one hand on the sheet on the other side of her, his hip hard against her silk covered flank. 'Eight *p.m,* kitten . . . we have the whole night ahead of us . . .'

'You let me sleep the clock around?' she whispered shakily.

'You needed it.'

'Weren't you afraid I'd wake up and run off while you were at work?' she taunted, not trusting his benevolence.

'You couldn't run far or fast enough. But as it happens I didn't go down to the office. I had my secretary cancel my appointments and send my paperwork up here.'

He had chosen her over his *bank*? The implications made Kat dizzy. 'Oh, Daniel . . .' He had tended her wound, watched over her . . .

He picked up her left hand, entwining her fingers with his. 'You're not wearing Todd's ring. Did you argue after I stormed out on you? Did you argue about me?'

'I . . . yes . . . but——'

'Good.' His husky satisfaction roughly shouldered aside her weak attempt to explain. There was a world of knowledge and experience in the eyes that lowered to where her other hand held the sheet. 'I can make you forget him, Kathleen. I can make you forget every other man you've ever known. I'll fill you so full of me that there's no room for anyone or anything else . . .'

And to prove that the satiny vow wasn't an idle boast, he kissed her, but not on the lips that tingled for his possession. Instead he gently plucked her hand from the sheet and, as the silk slithered into her lap, he bent and sweetly nuzzled against her breasts. Kat went rigid with shock and delight at the light caress of his tongue, and the small sound she made in her throat encouraged him to be bold. He cupped her firmly, thumbs rubbing slowly back and forth across her nipples as they left the moist cavern of his mouth. She moaned, taking his head in her hands, cradling him in an agony of bliss.

By the time he kissed her mouth she was starving for the taste of him and, like a drug, she discovered she needed more and more of him to sustain her high. She hardly felt him toss back the sheet and stroke his hands up her long, golden legs, or heard him murmur with pleasure at what he found. She was awash with pure sensation, the slide of silk beneath her, the brush of his sweater against her sensitised breasts and belly, the musky male scent of him seducing her willing heart and mind.

'That's right, kitten . . . burn for me, ache for me . . .' he whispered as he nipped her skin. 'This is what I've been thinking about all day, why I couldn't concentrate . . . I was thinking of you, waiting for me in my bed . . . But we're not going to hurry. We have all night, and the first time should always be slow and easy . . . a glorious, long-drawn-out agony of sighs.' He parted her thighs and touched her with exquisite intimacy. She trembled, wishing it wasn't really her first time, wishing that she had more to give him, was capable of matching him touch for experienced touch, wishing that she was so skilled in the art of giving pleasure that she would exist forever within him, a permanent kink in his libido that would spoil other women for him . . . and him for other women . . .

He took devilish delight in eluding her passionately eager attempts to hurry the pace, drawing away from her to undress, standing beside the bed, stripping slowly, lazily, every movement a sexual tease. Without his clothes he looked bigger, more muscled, his masculinity raw, unrefined by the sleek tailoring that usually muted its impact. His sculpted chest was thick with silver-flecked black hair, and further down, below the hard-packed waist, the scattering of hair thickened again, a dark cradle for his manhood. Kat felt the beginnings of panic. How could she have dared imagine that she could satisfy him? How did she make this special for him—as special as it was for her?

As if he sensed her uncertainty, he shed the pretence of laziness and joined her on the bed, his body flexing and tightening as he shifted over her, supporting his weight on rigid arms, shuddering slightly as her hands moved exploringly over the hard ridges of bone and muscle on his strongly braced back.

'How you excite me,' he whispered thickly. 'I said slow and easy, my beautiful kitten, but I don't know if I can deliver——'

'Oh, please don't,' she pleaded blindly. 'I want to have it all . . . please, Daniel . . . *now* . . . love me . . .'

And he did, lowering himself to her, moving, skin on skin, rocking, thrusting, sliding against her until there was no part of her that didn't know him, didn't welcome him.

And yet, in spite of her passionate response, when the moment came he was conscious of her infinitesimal withdrawal. He controlled it easily, but it wasn't until he completed his first, slow thrust that he realised the reason for it. By then it was too late for regrets, and her soundless sigh of wonder made them redundant. Gritting his teeth, Daniel strove to restrain his explosive joy, moving his hips very delicately until his selflessness drove him to the edge of madness and his control faltered, then shattered completely when Kat began to shudder beneath him, crying his name in wild triumph and fearful ecstasy. They plunged together into blackness shot with blinding bolts of lightning, another dimension, frighteningly alien, terrifyingly beautiful, beyond any dream of pleasure.

Only after her shaking stopped and her stunned muscles were flooded with flowing lassitude did he withdraw with a soft groan of regret. He turned on his side, cupping her jaw with a possessive hand.

'You haven't slept with him—Todd—or any other man. This was your first time.' His voice still held a lingering shock.

'I . . . was I that obvious?' Kat murmured, still half dazed by the glory of it all.

'You were marvellous.' He sensed the underlying insecurity. 'But just a little too tense, a little too tight, and a little too startled by what happened to you. 'The love-blush on her skin deepened and he laughed tenderly.' I'm rather enchanted and very, very flattered. It was all I could do to slow down so I wouldn't hurt you. I had to feel you take all of me . . . your first man.' There was an intensely masculine triumph in his words. Then, within a heartbeat, he managed to destroy the bliss he had created in her mind and body. 'Are you going to tell Todd, or do you want me to talk to him?'

Kat stiffened. 'W-what do you mean?' She felt as if she had been drenched in cold water. Had her supreme act of love been wasted? Was this to Daniel just a means to an end?

His eyes narrowed as he placed his own swift interpretation on her rigid shock. 'This changes everything, doesn't it?'

'Does it?' she whispered painfully, bracing herself for what was to come. Oh, surely he hadn't plannned all this for *Todd's* sake? All that tenderness and passion . . . had it all been a fake, a fraud?

There was no sign of either of those things in his face now. His jaw was tight, his eyes hard, his body menacingly still. 'Surely you can't mean to carry on as if *this* never happened?' An angry gesture indicated the tumbled bed.

'Is that why you seduced me?' she asked wretchedly, pulling her lovely castle of dreams down around her ears.

'We seduced each other, Kathleen,' he corrected her brutally. 'You may have been a virgin, but you were with me every step of the way.'

Kat's silent scream of pain echoed in the hollow chambers of her heart, but she was too proud to let him see the extent of his victory and her shame. Her face was a mask of cold beauty as she reached for the sheet to cover their nakedness. She dared not try and get out of bed for fear she would collapse weeping on the floor.

Her silence as much as her rigid indifference condemned her. Daniel was sickened at how close he had come to falling into her trap, enraged by the raw sense of betrayal that tore through him. He should have known better than to trust his instincts where a beautiful, wanton woman were concerned—for she had certainly been that, in spite of her virginity. The old wound began to throb anew. Would he never learn? The desire for revenge bit deep. She had used her body to win favours from him . . . well, she was going to get more than she had bargained for. She had made her bed—with him—and, dammit, that was where she was going to lie . . . at least until he had slaked his appetite for her flesh, used her as she had used him. Her continued silence, those huge accusing eyes as if *he* were the betrayer

rather than she, goaded him into slashing them both with
ruthless cruelty.

'And they were irrevocable steps, Kathleen. Even if Todd
could bring himself to take my leavings, I'm damned if any
ex-lover of mine is going to marry another member of my
family!'

Ex-lover. The sneer was like a stake through her aching
throat, locking her into speechless agony. She shook her
head, tumbled curls a glowing frame for her bleached face,
shattered by the knowledge that, in his oh-so-very-thorough
fashion, Daniel had planned the end of their affair even as it
began!

'I hold all the cards, don't force me to play them,' he
threatened her denial rawly. 'You've made your choice—me
—and now I'm going to make you abide by it. It's over
between you and Todd. Not even an infatuated fool like
him would forgive you this, not after I've finished telling
him the way it was.'

'How can something be over when it doesn't even exist?'
Kat finally found her voice, cracked and harsh, to fling
down her joker, the wild card that rendered his unbeatable
hand useless. It poured out of her, the naked truth, all
except that last, too-revealing conversation with Sharon.
Only by humiliating him did Kat feel that she could ease
her own humiliation, hide her excruciating vulnerability.

Only, as so often had happened before, she had under-
estimated Daniel. His reaction wasn't at all what she had
expected. Oh, there was a brief, molten flare of rage, but
that swiftly congealed into something infinitely more
dangerous—a clever, calculating intelligence—and he began
to laugh.

'You think it's funny that you've been played for a fool?'
she demanded of him, furious that he wasn't crushed.

'Ah, but you were too . . . such delicious irony. Of course,
I knew . . .'

'You *knew*?' Kat was outraged.

'Not the extent of it . . . but certainly that there was more going on than met the eye. Didn't I tell you that I'd get it out of you?' He was gloating now, his smile almost sensuous in its curve of angry admiration. His eyes pinned her to the bed, reinforcing her belief that she had made a terrible mistake in blurting out the truth. 'So there was never anything between you and Todd, it was all a lie, a manipulating lie. And I fell for it, all the way . . . I even found myself beginning to trust your integrity. I bet that amused you, Kathleen. But you're not laughing now, are you? *I'm* the one enjoying the joke . . .'

Hypnotised by his softness of voice, Kat was taken by surprise when he suddenly ripped the sheet away from her white-knuckled hands. She gasped and tried to cover herself, but he was there first, trapping her hands on either side of her head. 'And what was this supposed to achieve, I wonder?' he asked, still with deadly softness, as he surveyed her trembling body, still bearing the marks of his possession. 'Was I supposed to be so overcome with guilt at the besmirching of your innocence that I begged for the honour of your pure hand in marriage? Or was I merely supposed to be so intoxicated by your charms that I'd blindly let you wreck the rest of my life? Who choreographed this première performance between the sheets, my dear? Todd? My sister?'

'Don't be disgusting!'

'No,' the certainty blazed in his eyes as he ignored her interruption, 'of course not. You're here, my beautiful cheat, for the same reason I am. You couldn't help yourself. At some very basic level we have a greed for each other that I don't think one bite at the forbidden fruit is going to satisfy, do you?'

He stroked her, and her heart shuddered beneath the breast that peaked to his caress, the hand that he had freed frozen by a dart of joy. He couldn't help himself? So it *wasn't* planned? It *had* been real, what they shared? And she had ruined the precious aftermath with her mistrust!

He was moving over her now. 'So we're going to gorge

ourselves, Kathleen, until we've stripped the tree. But from here on in *I* make the rules. Understand, I won't allow you to control me with sex or guilt. Outside this bedroom you have no influence over me. When and whom I marry is no business of yours, or my family's. I shall do as I please in my own time, in my own way. And at the moment, this is what pleases me.' His fingers moved up her thigh and touched, and he smiled at what he found. 'Remember how good it was the first time, kitten? The second is always better, more intense.' This time his movement was forceful, direct, and she uttered a soft moan as his muscles bunched, his inner turmoil adding an explosive element to his renewed desire. She understood his need to punish, even welcomed it in the hope that it would go some way to repairing the rent to his pride, but his next words fired her own.

'You'll enjoy being my mistress, Kathleen, as long as you play by the rules. And the first one is that a mistress's loyalty belongs to her master. From now on, you only play the roles that *I* assign you.'

'Oh, no, Daniel Bishop,' Kat couldn't let him dominate her completely, but she loved him too much to pass up this chance of redemption, the only opportunity she might get to burrow into his life . . . to lay siege to his sequestered heart, 'not your mistress. I'll be your lover, yes, but I'll never, *never* be your mistress!'

He growled an angry laugh as he took her. To hell with semantics. At last he had her exactly where he wanted her . . . didn't he?

CHAPTER NINE

'CHECKMATE.'

Daniel shook his head sharply and looked down at the chessboard. His eyebrows rose in surprise.

'How the hell did that happen?'

'I guess you just weren't concentrating,' said Kat kindly.

His pride refused the offer. He studied the evidence of his downfall for a few more seconds before he stiffened. Incredulous blue eyes shot up to duel with her innocent ones.

'You cheated!'

'My goodness, Daniel, you are a sore loser.'

'You cheated!' he insisted in a tone of high offence. 'You switched some pieces.'

'Nonsense. How could I have done when you've been sitting there the whole time? You should be flattered that you lost, since you taught me everything I know about chess. You told me that the whole point of chess is to take advantage of your opponent's weaknesses——'

'*Within* the rules of the game.' Daniel's sternness was tempered by exasperated amusement. 'That doesn't include sneaking pieces off the board when he isn't looking. That bishop you used in the mate was a pawn a few minutes ago.'

'The only Bishop I needed to use was the one on the other side of the board,' Kat grinned. 'Shall we call it a draw?'

'No.' They measured stubborn gazes. 'Not until you admit you cheated.'

'I'm not going to admit I cheated until you admit you weren't concentrating.'

'I wasn't concentrating.'

'I cheated.'

He laughed at her prompt confession. 'I suppose if I

didn't notice, then I *deserved* to lose.'

'Quite,' said Kat smugly.

'Well, you have my undivided attention now,' he said, showing that he understood the reason for her pique. Daniel was rarely so abstracted in her presence. Even when he was working on his clocks and she was curled up in a corner with a book, he was usually aware of the exact moment she became restless.

'Why the mighty frowns? Trouble at t'bank?' she adopted a broad, North-of-England accent. 'Or at home?'

A month ago she wouldn't have dared to ask. A month ago he would have put her very firmly in her place. But, as Kat had hoped, Daniel had been unable to sustain his stranglehold on their affair. How could he use someone who refused to feel used? How could he take from someone who gave with such passionate generosity?

At first her pride had taken a battering, although she had tried hard not to show it. Daniel had worked long hours and had a full quota of social engagements to attend—always, of course, with the incomparable Clarissa on his arm. Sometimes, even on the nights that he went to a dinner or show with his fiancée, Kat would receive a late-night phone call or, if she was at the theatre or at Gino's, there would be flowers and a note, and after she had finished work she would slip away to find Seth waiting to drive her to the apartment. She knew it was Daniel's way of paying her back for insisting on moving in with a friend rather than letting him set her up in an apartment somewhere. As soon as Stanton Street had become habitable again, she had returned there to the support, and tacit disapproval, of her flatmates. She had returned each and every gift that Daniel gave her. Only flowers didn't violate her pride. She wanted no hint of commercial transaction to tarnish her loving—nothing he could throw in her face later.

It had taken a few weeks, but gradually Daniel's fierce resistance against anything but a purely sexual relationship had waned. Their affair was still conducted within the strict limits of secrecy, but they were spending more and more of their time together out of bed—talking, learning from and about each other. Kat restrained her wild hope with caution, careful not to make any demand on him that he could interpret as an assumption of power. The only power she was confident of exercising over him was one of fascination. At the moment she held his interest. She must build on that. What the future held she dared not think of, but if he could love her here and now perhaps the future would take care of itself. Daniel's cynicism, his experience of love, both familial and romantic, made him slow to trust, but she knew that that trust, once given, was irrevocable. No wonder he extended the gift so sparingly.

With a sweeping gesture Daniel scattered the chess pieces from the board and lay back on the thick, gold-flecked carpet, head propped up on his hand. The evening sun, slanting in through the penthouse windows behind him, gave him an improbable halo to contradict the silver horns. Playing on the floor was his concession to Kat, who preferred to sprawl. She was an erratic player at best, and if she was going to lose, as she invariably did, she at least deserved to do it in comfort!

'Trouble at home. An almighty row. Adelaide has discovered that Sharon has been seeing some man on the sly—a music teacher she met at her music group. Apparently it has become rather serious. Adelaide wants me to find out what he wants and warn him off.'

'Oh.' Kat bit the inside of her cheek, concentrating on picking up the chess pieces and packing them back into their box. Therefore she didn't see Daniel's expectant expression change to one of disappointment.

'Aren't you going to venture an opinion?'

'Why should I?'

'Because you and Sharon, and Diana too, are still very thick. I don't suppose that what was news to Adelaide and I is news to you. In fact, I wouldn't be surprised if it wasn't *you* who encouraged Sharon to bring it out into the open.'

Kat's chin jerked up. The defiant impulse died when she saw the mixture of amusement and resignation in his blue eyes. He didn't look as if he was about to reiterate his injunction that she was to stay away from his family. Diana had reported a spine-chilling encounter session with Daniel following her exposure of their plot. In the heat of the moment Kat hadn't considered the consequences to her friends, but Diana told her they had all been verbal. 'He threatened to tell Mother about our heresy if we even *thought* about meddling in his life again. Kąt, we positively *grovelled*—base cowards to the last!'

'I just said that it was better you found out from her than from some other busybody. Stephen's a lovely man.'

'You've met him?' She nodded. 'He's divorced with two teenage daughters.' His voice was neutral but Kat stiffened defensively.

'Who live with him and are great girls. They adore Sharon, and you know how she's always wanted a daughter.' After Todd, Sharon had suffered a pelvic inflammation that had led to a hysterectomy. 'Dammit, at least meet the man, Daniel, before you start throwing out bribes. He may not be rich, but he makes a comfortable living and has his own home. He can make Sharon happy—he loves her—but perhaps that doesn't matter much in your scheme of things——' She allowed a little of her own bitterness to escape the tight net of her emotions.

'You don't have a very good opinion of my personal integrity, do you, Kathleen?' he said quietly.

'Of course I do!' She was startled by the suggestion. 'It's just——'

'That you consider me weak-willed and easily led. Firmly tied to my mother's apron-strings.'

'Don't be ridiculous!' she snapped.

'I'm not. That's what your opinion boils down to. You don't trust me to put Sharon's welfare ahead of my own.'

'Of the *family's*,' Kat corrected him.

'We're not the Mafia, Kathleen.'

'Tell that to your mother.'

'Maybe if you tried to understand her, rather than just condemn her——'

'The way she condemns others, you mean?'

'Yes.' Daniel's continued quietness penetrated her rising anger. 'I thought you were different, Kathleen. Why can't you extend your compassion for the underdog to *all* those who deserve it, regardless of rank or privilege? Are you jealous of Adelaide?'

'Of course not,' said Kat truthfully, not liking his comparison. *Had* she been as arrogant, in her own way, as Adelaide?

'No. Why should you be? You live exactly the way you please. She, on the other hand, has a number of reasons to be jealous of *you*.'

Kat scrambled to her feet, wounded by what she saw as his sarcasm. Daniel followed her, quick to empathise. Too quick. He made her feel impossibly vulnerable to his perception.

'I'm serious,' he said, his hands settling on her shoulders as she stood, staring out at the roof garden. 'Don't you realise that one of the reasons Adelaide felt such antipathy towards you was that, in spite of the vulgarity you were deliberately exuding, she could see that you possessed something she has never had—the ability to be at ease with people, to inspire them to *like* you? People do like you, Kathleen—even when you're annoying the hell out of them. There's an intrinsic warmth in your nature which is literally irresistible.' He turned her to face him with a gentle pressure. 'My mother, on the other hand, has always had to work hard to acquire friends. She's an extremely proud woman and has always found it difficult to express emotion, and consequently she comes across as cold. It creates a vicious circle with her trapped inside it.

'I'll admit that Mother's snobbery is tiresome, but that's the way she was brought up, and her fixation with getting her own way is partly because of her basic insecurity as a person. She never had the freedom to discover herself, as you have. *What* she was was more important than *who* she was, and that can be crippling to the growth of self-esteem. For instance, I think Mother would have loved to organise something other than home and family and her various charities. She has a businesswoman's brain, but the rigid expectations of her era and class closed off that option. Neither her father nor mine approved of women working just for the sake of it. All that energy and intelligence, and no emotional outlets . . . it's not surprising that she's desperate to retain what power she does have over the rest of us. Father's and Sean's deaths deprived her of a valuable part of her power base, as well as of a husband and son. Sean was her favourite, and for a few years she resented me for his death. I was the prodigal son, the unknown quantity—as an adult, anyway—coming home to steal all the power and glory . . .'

'So you paid for the crime of profiting from your brother's death by becoming part of her power base,' said Kat, with sudden insight. Love and guilt, the great hidden motivators.

He shrugged, wryly, his hands absently caressing her arms. 'Part of me is very comfortable with the rules of behaviour that she insists on. After all, I was brought up to obey them. To me, they're just a kind of game, to Mother they're real . . . that's the difference between us. I tried to get her more involved at the bank once, through Todd's proxy, but she's too old to change. She feels safe in her world. Any changes will have to come from without rather than from within, and she'll fight them every inch of the way. Change is something she can't control, you see . . .'

'How sad,' Kat murmured, and he smiled, a hand moving to cup her face.

'Don't start feeling too sorry for her; she won't thank you for it. I just wanted you to understand why I allow her a certain . . . latitude. I don't parrot her prejudices and opinions, but I can't dismiss them as of no account. I know she has no other outlets for her frustrations. I have plenty for mine . . . this apartment, my collection, my art, my mistress . . .' He smiled wickedly.

He had meant to be teasing, but unfortunately the word as well as the context struck a tender spot. Was that all she was, *still*—an outlet for his frustrations? She jerked away from his hold. 'I'm not your anything. I'm my own woman, and don't you ever forget it!'

'How could I? You remind me every time you get out of my bed.' It was a bone of contention that she would never *sleep* with him. She always made herself leave his arms, whatever the hour, to go home to sleep. It was too dangerous to think of her happiness as secure in his arms.

'You made the bed, you lie on it.'

'Even if it's a bed of nails?' His mouth had quirked ironically at her words, as if he was remembering something.

'You pay your money and you take your choice, Daniel,' Kat said tartly, to hide her leap of expectation.

'In this case there is no choice. Kat, I don't want to marry Clarissa, but——'

But I'm going to. Kat didn't want to hear it. 'Oh, come on, Daniel, if you're going to start shedding crocodile tears about how your wife doesn't understand you even *before* the fact——'

'But she does, admirably. That's the *point*.'

'A compliant wife, how lucky for you! But don't look to me, Daniel Bishop, to join you in complicity. A *ménage à trois* is not my scene.'

'Nor mine,' he said crisply. 'Kathleen, I can't explain yet, but there are reasons——'

'Of course there are,' drawled Kat, injecting a note of boredom into her voice, 'and I'm sure they're quite splendid . . .'

Daniel's blue eyes narrowed impatiently. 'Reginald Paine and I have some very intricate business connections. At the moment the bank is negotiating a directorship on one of his companies——'

'And his daughter is part of the package deal,' Kat finished for him. 'Yes, I see. How awkward for you. How self-sacrificing.' Her flippancy had angered him, so she played to the advantage. Damn him, she didn't want to know any good reason he had to marry Clarissa, business or otherwise, and his seriousness frightened her badly. He had told her that first night that he wasn't sleeping with his fiancée, taunting Kat that when he did her services would no longer be required. Now, it seemed, he had changed his mind, but Kat hadn't. She loved him too much to degrade that love in adultery.

'If you'd let me finish——'

'Oh, don't be such a *bore* about it, Daniel. It's not as if it really matters to *us*. I'm just along for the ride, remember? I'm not into anything deep and meaningful at this point in my life. I don't want to lock myself into any dead-end relationship when I know there's something, some*one* better for me out there.'

'Are you trying to tell me that you're seeing someone else?' Daniel demanded, having gone from impatience to frozen rage in the space of five sentences.

From his expression, she judged she would be unwise to lie. 'Of course not! Unlike you, I do have some sense of morality left. Besides, when would I get *time*? If I'm not here I'm at the theatre, or sleeping at home, or at Gino's or at a seminar.' She had attended several of late, on the subjects of economics and investment, building up the knowledge to complement the rare, instinctive 'feel' she had discovered for turning a fast buck. Much to Daniel's awed amusement, and the horror of the stockbroker he had recommended she use, her erratic, intuitive buying and selling of shares had already netted her a tidy sum. Kat wondered whether she had perhaps stumbled on her true vocation: that of fat-Kat capitalist! It was fun, more profitable than performing and, to Kat, more of a challenge.

Daniel's icy anger died as swiftly as it had been born.

'You don't have to put yourself through all that, Kathleen.'

'Don't start that again.' Her eyes sparked warningly at him and he sighed.

'When are you going to start giving me the benefit of the doubt?

'When there's something to doubt. I know what this "I'm only marrying for business reasons" is all about, and I'll only say this once: I don't sleep with married men!'

'You should wait until you're asked,' he said, with more than a hint of hauteur, although a strange smile danced at the corners of his sensual mouth, half mocking, half wistful. 'If I ever do, you might find there are exceptions to every rule.'

'Not this one,' she snarled, and he made a muffled sound of exasperation and suddenly caught her by the waist, swinging her around with effortless strength.

'Come with me.'

She dug her heels in, inwardly weeping at his insensitivity, determined to match it with a crudity of her own.' I don't feel like sex right now, Daniel.'

'You have a one-track mind, my sweet.' He grinned at her and she flushed as she saw he was dragging her towards his studio rather than the bedroom.

When he had first shown her his studio, she had been stunned. They had been having a heated difference of opinion about modern art, and she had accused him of possessing the artistic sensibility of a rogue elephant. No wonder he hadn't made it as an artist, she had jeered.

'Watercolours? These are *yours?*' she had blurted disbelievingly as she had surveyed the very un-Daniel litter of paint and canvas, so different from the precision of his other workroom. Around the walls were many paintings, framed and unframed—small, delicate, impressionistic works done in subtle washes of colour. She leaned closer to one. 'That's not your name.'

'I sell through the gallery of a friend. And I use a pseudonym because I prefer to sell through artistic merit rather than publicity value,' he said, matter-of-factly.

'But . . . *watercolours*?' When Kat thought of Daniel in her mind, it was in terms of primary colours and strong lines.

'Doesn't fit in with your stereotype image of me, does it?' He had not hidden his satisfaction at having surprised her yet again. 'What did you expect—big, bad, bold oils brimming with all the savage emotions that have to be repressed in my daily life?'

She had, and she admitted it cheerfully, entranced by the reality. These paintings were from Daniel's heart as much as from his brain, she realised delightedly—discipline and love perfectly married. Why couldn't he allow himself that outside his art?

'Is this the kind of work you did in Europe?'

'No. Actually I specialised in big, bad, bold oils brimming with savage emotions,' he confessed wryly.

She laughed. 'So why the switch?'

'An experiment. Then, too, there was my change of life-style. I no longer had the time to spend days, weeks . . . even months labouring over a single painting . . . I needed a more instant form of artistic gratification. Then there's the challenge. It's much more difficult to touch people with softness and subtlety than it is with boldness and brilliance of colour. Delicacy, unfortunately, has become almost a lost cause in the current trend of modern art . . . these days the message must leap out of the medium. It's challenging, too, to try and get something right first time. With oils you can paint over a mistake. A watercolour stands or falls on each stroke of the brush.'

'They're beautiful,' said Kat wonderingly, as she moved around the room. 'How could you bear to give it up?'

'But I haven't.' He indicated the cluttered room.

'You know what I mean. To have to relegate such talent to just a corner of your life . . .'

'Ah, Kathleen, surely you of all people should understand,' he murmured gently. 'Having the talent to do something doesn't necessarily mean that one has the ambition or dedication to carry it through to its natural conclusion.'

'It's not the same thing,' she denied, strangely shocked at the suggestion of affinity.

'I enjoy success with my painting, but I don't *need* it. It's not a driving force in my life. It never was. At one time I took it seriously, but that was in the nature of an experiment, and at the same time the perfect medium for rebellion against a strait-laced family. I find painting both relaxing and stimulating, but there's not the inner compulsion there, Kat, that distinguishes a good artist from a great one. I can run the bank and paint on the side. The reverse isn't possible. This way I get to have my cake and eat it, too . . .'

'What are you doing?' Kat shook herself back to the present to find Daniel busily unbuttoning her mint jumpsuit, legacy of another hilarious shopping expedition, this time *within* her budget, with his sister and sister-in-law.

'You can't wear that, it's too concealing.'

'I'm not posing in the nude,' she said half-heartedly, flattered.

'I don't want you to,' he said, to her chagrin. 'Put this on. It should fit. Your friend Freya gave me your measurements.'

'This' was a flounced white dress of broderie anglaise with a scooped, elasticised neckline that bared her shoulders. Kat put it on as Daniel set up his easel and sketching materials, and found that it did indeed fit . . . beautifully. When Daniel turned around to arrange her pose, the tender look in his eyes made her feel weak. At times like this she could almost believe that he was falling in love with her.

'You look about sixteen,' he said huskily. 'It was supposed to make you look sultry, not sweet and innocent. Come and sit down.' He held the padded velvet chair as she sat down, his hands lingering on the smooth slope of her shoulders as he ruffled her hair into a disordered mane. 'You make me feel like a dirty old man,' he groaned as he wrestled with his baser impulses. He had brought her here to paint her, not to make love to her.

'You *are* a dirty old man, Daniel,' she told him sweetly, unsure of what to make of his desire to paint her. He would be using oils, of course—she had noticed the stack of portraits in the corner—most of them women, executed in a variety of styles. Was she another experiment? Was this the artistic equivalent of collecting locks of hair as mementoes of one's conquests? 'Am I to join your female rogues' gallery, or are you going to flog me off to the highest bidder?' she asked jokingly.

'That's up to you.' Daniel was already absorbed in his task, sketching her from various angles. 'Since you wouldn't let me give you a present on your birthday, perhaps you'll consider the fruits of my sweated labour an acceptable substitute.'

Kat hesitated. 'Thank you.' The row over the Cartier watch he had bought for her had spoiled her birthday. Perhaps she *was* being too stubborn about her golden rule. Perhaps she should see his attempted generosity not as the thin end of the wedge, but as a genuine attempt to free their relationship . . .

Ten minutes later, when Daniel casually suggested she keep the dress, too, since he would have no use for it after the portrait was finished, all Kat's suspicions snapped back into place. Another wounding argument ensued, Daniel frustrated and Kat angered by his skill at putting her obscurely in the wrong.

That day seemed to mark an uneasy turning point in their affair. For the next few weeks, as the end of summer began to fade into autumn, their roles became strangely reversed. Daniel advanced, Kat retreated. The more pressure he put on her to respond to him, the more afraid she was to expose herself to him. She was being wooed, rather forcibly, but she knew now that she was being wooed as a mistress.

It was a subtle, seductive form of power play—with Daniel, the master, at his best. It took all Kat's strength to resist, to preserve her shaky self-respect in the face of his persistent attempts to undermine it. Withholding her love was essential to her precarious defences, the blind courage with which she had embarked on their affair draining away just when she needed it most. Daniel seemed to be devouring her every waking thought. In a few short months she had changed into a person she hardly recognised any more . . . and whom she wondered whether she liked. She was even afraid that her newfound pleasure in the idea of a career in investments was but a subconscious attempt to gain her lover's approval. Daniel's wooing assiduously avoided any false promises, and Kat despised herself for wanting them. She suddenly wanted it over with. Nothing could be worse than this half-life of faded dreams . . .

One evening Daniel made love to her in the rain, on the little patch of grass protected by the tall trees in their pots. Every moment was precious now, a memory to be stored against the winter to come, and their lovemaking had taken on a new edge that sharpened her senses. At least with her body she could lavish him with love. The rain slanted down in earnest, slicking Daniel's hair as he rose above her, running in rivulets down his rippling back and chest as he moved between her parted thighs, but still he did not stop.

Afterwards he carried her chilled body inside and laid her on the carpet while he found an enormous scented bath-towel and used it to arouse her all over again. His movements this time were slow and languorous, and when he had finished she was no longer chilled but flushed and trembling, achingly satisfied. He wrapped her in one of his robes and put on a matching one for himself, and they drank brandy among the scattered clothes and damp towels. With his hair still slicked back Daniel looked more relaxed than she had ever seen him, and . . . somehow . . . defenceless. Kat felt all her resistance give under the weight of her love. To hell with pride. She wanted him to know . . .

'Daniel——' She cupped his hard jaw, and he turned his mouth submissively against her palm.

'You taste of me,' he murmured huskily. 'I like that . . .'

'Oh, Daniel, I——'

The sound of the lift doors was an ugly shock. No one came up in the private lift uninvited, or without clearance from security. Daniel rolled quickly to his feet and stiffened.

'Clarissa!'

'Daniel.' After the first instant of dismay, the classical features rapidly readjusted themselves into seamless blandness. 'Hello, Kathleen.' Kat had to admire her poise. The greeting was without the faintest vestige of sarcasm or embarrassment.

'Clarissa, this is . . . unexpected.' The master of understatement was equally quick to recover. Two of a kind, thought Kat helplessly. She rose awkwardly, internally cringing at the situation.

'I'm sorry for interrupting.' Clarissa cast a cool, blank look at the incriminating evidence, and by accident Kat caught her eyes as she looked away. Her heart stopped in her chest. The glitter in those empty eyes! *Tears*? Clarissa's beautiful face was still smooth, but Kat suddenly identified the tension coming off her in waves. Panic. Fear.

'Clarissa?' The gentle note in Daniel's voice brought her heart thunderingly to life. Oh, no . . . he had lied. Daniel had lied when he had claimed there was only business between them. No man could look at a woman like that, speak in that tender voice, and not be involved. It bespoke an intimacy and trust that Kat had never dreamed existed. It made her feel sick and ashamed of what she had done, what she was doing . . .

'I'm sorry,' Clarissa repeated with a controlled smile that fooled no one.' I asked the guard to key the lift for me. I'm afraid it didn't occur to me that you might have someone here.' She spread her hands, actually *apologising,* but Kat observed with horror that the long, graceful, exquisitely kept hands were trembling. 'I needed to see you . . . rather urgently. I need to talk to you . . .'

'Of course. Kathleen, would you mind?' The formal request was a dismissal that put her firmly in her place. Clarissa, she realised tiredly, would always come first. In the monumentally selfish arrogance of her love, it had pleased Kat to see her as a cipher, an insignificant rival compared to Daniel's own determined rejection of love as a basis for marriage. She had been wrong. If Daniel wore a mask in public, why not Clarissa, too? And behind their masks was a bond that they obviously knew they could rely on.

'Kat?' Daniel's voice was harsh, demanding, nothing like the patient tone he used with his fiancée. His eyes were unreadable, and Kat knew him well enough to know that it meant he was angry. 'You understand, don't you?'

'Yes. I understand.' More than he knew.

It was over. Before, it had been possible to pretend that she was hurting no one. Now the pathetic pretence was laid bare. He had never made her any false promises. She had no right to feel betrayed. But she did.

Steadily she walked away from the beautifully matched couple, into the bedroom where she shakily pulled on her street clothes and began to gather up the small evidences of her visits to the apartment and tuck them into the soft-sided bag from the closet. She packed her economics text-books and a few odds and ends of clothes, the cosmetics and shampoo from the en suite bathroom and the joke pair of striped flannelette pyjamas that Daniel had ripped all the buttons off when she wore them to challenge his assertion that any kind of nightwear, except satin, silk and lace, was a turn-off. She had primly fought him when he quickly changed his mind, hence the damage. Then he had confiscated the trousers and made her wear the buttonless top, enjoying the contrast between the prosaic prudity of the loose jacket and the tantalising glimpses of naked flesh it afforded him when she moved.

Kat was zipping up the bag when Daniel entered the bedroom.

'You're leaving? Perhaps it's best.'

'I know it is,' said Kat grimly, taking one last look around the room where she had known so much happiness.

'This may take some time. I'll call you.'

Why? To prolong the agony of goodbye? 'Don't bother.'

'Kat?' He noticed the bag. 'What the hell's in there?'

'My things.'

'Dammit, Kat! I didn't mean that and you know it! Look, if you want to wait in here, that's fine. You don't *have* to go. But Clarissa's upset——'

'I can see that,' she said, tight-lipped, still refusing to look at him.

'Not about us. Something else . . . I can't explain.'

'I don't expect you to.' She tried to step around him, but he wouldn't let her. 'Let me go, Daniel.'

'No! Listen, let me ask Clarissa——'

'To leave?' Knowing he wouldn't. Knowing where his loyalty lay. She looked at him then, eyes full of golden scorn, and was savagely pleased to see his angry dismay as he thrust an impatient hand through his hair and glanced nervously behind him. 'It's a tough life, isn't it, Daniel, juggling two women? Rather appropriate, don't you think—me in the bedroom, her in the lounge? That sort of says it all doesn't it, about our little triangle?'

'Kathleen, it's not what you think——'

'You don't know what I think. You don't care what I think! I said I wasn't your mistress, but that's the way you've always thought of me, isn't it? Well, I've had it, Daniel. I'm bored with the set-up. Bored with the whole dead-end relationship!'

'What do you expect? I can't offer you anything else. Not——'

'Not with your fiancée sitting out in the lounge, no,' Kat

cut him off bitterly.

'Is that what you want, an offer of marriage? Is that what you've been holding out for?' he was goaded to reply.

'Don't worry. The only reason I'd ever marry is for *love*.'

'And of course you're not in love with me?'

Her stomach heaved. Was that what he wanted? The ultimate submission? She laughed harshly and turned her head blindly aside. His hand caught the nape of her neck and forced her eyes to his. 'Are you, Kathleen?' he demanded savagely.

Of course . . . he wanted to gloat. She had set out to ruin his marriage and had ruined herself instead . . . at least for any other man.

'No! I think you're contemptible!' she spat. 'Why don't you go back there to *her*? She's welcome to you.'

'And I mean nothing to you?'

'Nothing!' Her lips etched the lie, but her eyes were alight with a fury that reflected golden fires in his.

'Kathleen, you have to give me some time. Time to handle this, to discuss options with Clarissa,' he said with quiet urgency.

'Options?' She jerked convulsively in his grip, arching backwards against his hands, shivering with loathing, fighting the unbearable temptation of surrender. If she gave in, she would be lost forever. 'You bastard! I saw the way you looked at each other. You let me believe there was nothing between you.'

'I don't love her——'

'And that's supposed to make it all right to cheat on her?'

'It's not cheating. She *knows*.'

Kat felt faint. 'That makes it worse!' she choked.

'Kathleen, please, trust me.'

'*Trust* you?' Her mouth twisted in the parody of a laugh.

'Yes.' He shook her. 'You never have. You talk about *my* lack of trust, but when have you ever trusted me? Don't you know me *yet?*' The emphasis went over her head. 'Don't you know that I wouldn't ask for your understanding if I didn't know I was worthy of it? I can't tell you everything at the moment, but just give me a few minutes alone with Clarissa and I will. I promise. Please, for once, won't you trust me to do what's right?'

'Why?' Kat asked thickly, wavering. It was true. Even while she loved him, she expected the worst of him. Because it was safer that way, because all her life fantasies of the past had been safer than fantasies about the future. You couldn't protect yourself from the future as you could against the past. 'Why should I trust you?' Give me a reason I can *believe* . . .

He released her slowly, and stepped back. 'Perhaps because you owe it to me,' he murmured tiredly, with a cynical, humourless smile that questioned the words as he said them. 'Perhaps because I'm in love with you.'

If he hadn't qualified it; if he hadn't said it in that cynical tone of self-mockery; if his eyes hadn't been so cool, so guarded, so watchful, she might—just might —have allowed herself to believe the lovely fiction. She shook her head, denying the possibility. He couldn't love her, could he? He was just saying what he thought a woman wanted to hear, offering her a sop to her pride. If he loved her, why hadn't he told her *yesterday?*

And then it was too late, her silence too eloquent. The cool blue frost became wintry-grey pack-ice, freezing her out.

'Then there really is little point in staying. Go. Run

back to the security of your *friends*. And if you change your mind and want to come back, don't bother. I find you're not the woman I want, after all . . .'

CHAPTER TEN

KAT sat the jaunty red hat with its black half-veil on her sleek, French-pleated head and studied the effect. At least the veil disguised the dark circles under her eyes that make-up hadn't quite managed to hide, and softened the prominent hollows under her cheekbones.

'You look fantastic,' Freya sighed as Kat stood up and stepped back from the dressing-table to study the effect of an hour's work. 'Why is it that when *I'm* miserable I look like Dracula's bride, but *you* look mysterious and hauntingly beautiful?'

'As long as I look haunt*ing* and not haunt*ed*,' said Kat grimly. 'As the spectre at the feast, I want to see *him* haunted.'

Yes, the dress was just right. It was the same red as her hat, the deep wine-coloured shade that Daniel had once advised her to wear. The thin wool jersey was tailored yet feminine, designed to intimidate men who thought that a woman could only compete with them on their terms by adopting a certain masculinity. Smart business clothes were essential for inspiring confidence in her new job with a sharebroking and investment firm. Kat's employer had already told her that he was impressed by her potential, and she had taken that as sufficient encouragement to invest in an entirely new working wardrobe. Diana had helped, against Kat's initial protests. There was no reason, she had pointed out, for them not to be friends just because her brother was acting like a complete bastard. Why should Kat suffer any more than she already had? It was the right tack to take. Everything Kat did was aimed at proving, to herself and to Daniel Bishop, that she wasn't suffering.

Except, of course, she was . . .

Three weeks. Three weeks in which to decide that she had made a hideous mistake in burning her boats so thoroughly. She wanted Daniel back, but he wouldn't have her. The single conciliatory note she had tentatively sent resulted in nothing but a resounding silence. *Don't bother to come back*. She had done what she had sworn not to—given him an easy way out of their affair—and he had taken it.

Todd had told her sympathetically that Daniel was working like a demon on some special project, but the demon found plenty of time to be seen on the town with his fiancée, who seemed quite recovered from her quivering bout of weakness, Kat noticed with raging jealousy as she thumbed the financial pages to the gossip columns. Maybe that had been an act that Clarissa had put on to illustrate the hold she had on Daniel. Maybe Daniel had been in on it too . . . She remembered the lovemaking that had preceded the awful scene and decided, no. And Daniel had been too furious, justifiably so, she admitted now, with her stubborn refusal to trust him. She had been a coward and now she was paying the price.

Kat's hollow-eyed glance fell to the large, heavy, square envelope propped up on the dressing-table. Instant outrage! Her emotions had been all over the place for the last few weeks, and today was no exception. The swine! How dared he? How *dared* he?

It had come only this morning. Until the post had arrived, Kat had had no intention of going to the QueenCorp Annual General Meeting, being held at the Rex, Bishop building. When the invitation had come, she had immediately rung her broker to query it. Kevin Raymond was quick to disabuse her of the notion that she held no shares in the company.

'You have quite a nice chunk. I thought it was very clever of you, because most of the shares are in family hands. I'd love to know how you knew they were coming on the market.'

'I don't remember authorising any purchase,' frowned

Kat, who kept a close eye on her burgeoning portfolio.

'No? But it was only recent, Kat. Last week. You sent me a note with a bankers' draft to buy five thousand, and the name of the broker who was going to offer them.'

Kat blanched, her sweaty hand slipping on the receiver as the price of QueenCorp shares danced before her eyes. Nausea washed over her. Daniel! Who else was rich enough to make her such a contemptuous gift? She mumbled something and rang off. She could hardly explain to the curious Kevin that her former lover was the source of her clever investment, and that it was in the nature of a pay-off, designed to humiliate her. The amount was an insult, and intended as such . . . or was it supposed to be a consolation prize? *I don't want you, but you're welcome to a few crumbs from my table.* Kat's emotions seesawed wildly. One minute she wanted to stuff the shares down Daniel's arrogant throat, the next she wanted to build an empire on them and buy his bank from under him and grind *his* pride in the mud. Sometimes she thought she was going mad!

The visit to the doctor had calmed her down. He had told her about another one of Daniel's 'little gifts'. He had also chided her for her self-diagnosis of some sort of low-grade virus.

'In this enlightened age you should be ashamed of yourself! You're a bit run-down, but that's not surprising if you haven't adjusted your diet. I'll prescribe some iron tablets, but all you really need to do is make sure you're getting enough protein. You don't have to "eat for two", but if you're going to work right through your pregnancy you're going to need the body-builders rather than the cheaper forms of energy that carbohydrates and sugar provide. I'll give you a chart, if you like.'

Kat had accepted it numbly. About three and a half months, the doctor had said, and if Kat hadn't been dumbstruck she would have corrected him. Three months, three weeks and one day. That was how long it was since she and Daniel had made love for the first time. The only time they hadn't used any form of contraception.

She should have been devastated. Single, pregnant, abandoned by her lover—or as good as—and on the brink of a brand new career, Kat should have been as shocked and dismayed as her friends, to whom she had blurted out the incredible news. But she wasn't. For the first time in her life she would have someone of her own to love. Someone who wouldn't betray or abandon her. Someone who would love her as unconditionally as she loved him . . . or her. It gave her a sense of purpose, a core around which to shape the new life she was making for herself. At least she would have no financial worries! She would take the QueenCorp shares, after all. She would take them and put them in trust for her child. Daniel's child. *Their* child. He could marry Clarissa and her connections, and have a score of official Bishop heirs. But Kat, Kat would have his love-child, and that child would have all the love that she had not been allowed to give its father.

Or so were her virtuous thoughts, until that second invitation came, on the very morning of the AGM. The final straw.

She knew from the shape of the envelope that it was an invitation, and from the embossing on the back that it came from the Bishop household.

Her heart had begun to pound uncomfortably fast as she gingerly slid the stiff card from the envelope.

She stared, stricken, at the ornate cover of a wedding invitation. She opened it as if it contained a bomb. It did. She only had time to read 'Mrs Adelaide Bishop is pleased to request the presence of Kathleen Kendon at the wedding of . . .' before she staggered into the bathroom to retch in the basin, tears blurring out what she didn't want to see.

Oh, Kat didn't doubt that Adelaide was pleased. Whose idea was it to send out that invitation—hers or Daniel's? Had Adelaide got wind of their affair? Was this her way of trumpeting her victory? It must be. She refused to believe that Daniel would ever be so cruel. He had, after all,

tried to let her down gently, hadn't he? Had pleaded for
more time to bring their affair to a more amicable end.
Todd had once said that all Daniel's former lovers were his
friends. Well, not this one! This one was steaming mad!
How dared he? How *dared* he rush into marriage after all
this time? She saw no humour in the contradiction.

It was too much. She had crumpled the dreadful missive
in her hand and crammed it back into its bland envelope.
Before the astonished eyes of her friends, the sweetly
resigned madonna had transformed into an avenging angel.

'He needn't think he's getting away that easily!' she had
cried, rummaging furiously in her battered wardrobe.

'What are you going to do?' Colleen was frantically
signalling Freya, probably suggesting calling for a good
psychiatrist. 'You're not going to do anything stupid, are
you, Kat?'

'Of course not. I'm just going to see the father of my child
and demand he fulfil his parental obligations,' Kat had said
grimly, and her friends had subsided. They knew that there
was no arguing with Kat when she used that crusading tone
of voice. They had missed it of late, and welcomed
practically anything that would lift Kat out of a state of
miserable hibernation studded with erratic moods. Kat in
love, they agreed, was worse than the rest of them put
together!

'Now, are you sure you know what you're doing?' Freya
asked, as she handed Kat into the taxi that would ensure her
early arrival for the QueenCorp meeting.

'No. But I'm going to have fun doing it,' said Kat,
clutching the soft black bag through which she could feel
the sharp edges of Daniel's betrayal, that crumpled
invitation to cry at his wedding.

'Call if you need us,' said Colleen. 'If you're not back by
three, we'll send out a search party.'

'Remind them to drag the harbour.'

'You don't mean——' Freya looked horrified, and Kat
laughed for what seemed like the first time in weeks.

'Of course I don't. I've got the baby to think of now. But there's no telling what *he'll* do . . .' Go off the deep end, of course, accuse her of getting pregnant deliberately in order to manipulate him, ask her if she had any proof it was his. She deliberately shut off the memories of their last meeting, of Daniel telling her he loved her, with that cool, calculating look in his eye which invited disbelief. His brand of hidden love she could do without. Damn, now she was crying. Hormones, not Daniel, she told herself fiercely. She hated him and she was going to make him pay for hurting her.

The security man at the lift recognised her with a cheery wave, and Kat smiled grimly behind her veil. He might very well be removing her, kicking and screaming, within a very few minutes.

Daniel's secretary was less welcoming. 'I'm afraid Mr Bishop is busy right now.'

'I'm sure he'll spare time for me,' Kat lied sweetly.

'I'm sorry, but he has a QueenCorp AGM shortly—Mr Bishop is on the board, you know.' Kat didn't, but she wasn't surprised. Maybe she ought to report him for insider trading—*that* would cook his goose! 'In fact, he's with the chairman now,' his secretary interrupted her vengeful thoughts. 'I'm afraid he'll be tied up until—Miss Kendon——'

She was speaking to Kat's back. She hadn't come this far to be turned back at the mouth of the lion's den.

'Miss Kendon—Kathleen—you can't go in there——' The woman panted up behind her as Kat flung open the door. 'I'm terribly sorry, Mr Bishop,' she said frantically to the man behind the desk, 'but I just couldn't stop her.'

'Few people can,' Daniel murmured wryly, leaning back in his chair, narrowing his eyes to hide his elation. 'You're early, Kathleen.' He flicked a glance at her naked wrist. 'You should have kept the watch.' He watched her flush angrily and took his time looking over her, wanting her too furious to erect defences.

Kat ignored him. Her attention was centred on the two other people in the room—Reginald Paine and his daughter. So, QueenCorp was Reginald Paine's company! She relished, even more, the purpose to which his dividends would be put. He looked a pompous old bore, just right for Daniel's father-in-law. Clarissa, who had risen regally at the interruption, was looking quite subdued in a very plain grey suit with a pink silk blouse, but her smile at Kat was anything but. Of course, now that she had what she wanted, she had no reason to play damsel in distress.

Kat smiled back, eyes flashing tigerishly behind the veil as she turned to confront her prey.

'I need to talk to you rather urgently, Daniel,' she said in a sugar-sweet voice, watching his eyes narrow as he registered the very words that Clarissa had used that night in his apartment. Her tone, though, was very different . . . a silky threat contained in the sweetness.

'Daniel——' Reginald Paine frowned his impatience, and Kat braced herself for the first skirmish.

'Of course, Kathleen,' Daniel shocked at least two of his listeners with his swift compliance with what had been little more than a demand. Clarissa merely looked amused, which tightened Kat's temper another notch. 'Reginald, Clarissa . . . I'll see you downstairs shortly.' He glanced at his fob watch—a silver one, Kat noted absently—what had happened to his favourite gold?

Reginald Paine went, grumbling, throwing Kat a suspicious glance under his beetling brows, his daughter still with that callous smile that was salt in an open wound. The door closed behind them to a short silence.

'Well, Kathleen?'

Thank heaven for the partial concealment of her veil. She hoped the hunger in her eyes wasn't burning a hole through the net barrier. He was as beautiful as ever, seemingly untouched by the kind of dogged misery that had been Kat's lot this past month. His thick black hair was longer than she remembered, the silver devil's horns more

prominent than ever. In the black suit and white shirt and
pale yellow tie he looked formal and reserved, but Kat now
knew what lay beneath the mask. Daniel wasn't reserved,
merely well under control. She aimed to take some of that
control from him. She was too angry to be cautious, too
proud to be intimidated by his aura of power. She was a
successful woman in her own right, his equal in every way
that mattered.

'Drafting a marriage contract, were you? Or has that
already been signed and sealed?' Her first shot was across
his bows.

'Perhaps you'd better sit down.' He coolly deflected her
towards the chair his fiancée had so recently vacated.
Remembering the last time he had had her hovering at a
disadvantage, Kat thanked him nicely and made herself
comfortable, hoping the grinding of her teeth wasn't
audible.

'That's a stunning outfit, darling. Did you wear it to
impress me with your vibrant confidence?'

The casual endearment as much as his drawl infuriated
her, as if they were the merest of acquaintances. 'No, as a
matter of fact, this is my working gear.'

'Dressing for success? I understand you've made quite a
splash in financial circles,' he murmured.

'Don't be condescending, *darling*,' she told him fiercely.
'I *am* doing very well, and *I* didn't need the springboard of
a wealthy inheritance to do it, or the prop of an established
name. You'd better look to your back, Daniel; you may not
be as safe as you think you are.'

'Trying to frighten me, Kathleen? If you stab me, it will
be in the heart, from the front and I won't lift a finger to
stop you.' He held her suddenly uncertain gaze for a
moment. 'Are you here to demand I take those shares back?'

'If that's what you expected, you're going to be
disappointed. They'll come in very handy.'

Daniel showed his first sign of wariness. 'What are you
up to *now*?'

'Up to? Whatever can you mean?' Kat's nerves were beginning to jump and she savoured the feeling. She never felt so alive as when she was sparring with Daniel.

'I mean, I can't believe that you intend to let me off so easily. What are you going to do with the shares? Put them on the market at rock bottom and start a selling-fest? Or do you have some more personal revenge in mind?'

'Oh, it's very personal, Daniel,' she purred. She crossed her legs and watched his eyes fall to the slender length of thigh revealed by the movement. She recrossed them, sliding one leg sensuously down the other until he realised he was being teased and looked up, sapphire eyes darkened with unconcealed desire.

'Would it do any good to throw myself on your mercy?' he asked huskily. He looked as hungry as she had felt a few moments ago, and Kat swallowed, resisting the desire to leap across the desp and tear his clothes off and find the Daniel she had loved, the elemental man . . . the artist, the collector, the passionate lover, the man behind the image.

'After what you did?' She hardened her damaged heart.

'You were the one who walked out,' he pointed out. 'You were the one who wasn't prepared to work out our differences.'

'Is this what you call working it out?' She unzipped her clutch-bag with a vicious swipe and threw the crumpled envelope at him. It hit him on the chest and slid on to the white blotter in front of him. 'You didn't wait very long, did you, for a man who professed to be in love with me?'

'What's this?' He picked it up with such an expression of bewildered innocence that Kat nearly exploded.

'*That* is an invitation to the wedding!'

He grinned. *Grinned*. 'You got one, too? When, this morning?'

'Yes, this morning! Your mother's idea, I suppose, although I can't imagine that she actually expects me to accept. I might lower the tone of the proceedings. I suppose it was just a small piece of refined cruelty, the kind you

Bishops specialise in!'

He rose stiffly, his narrow face at last registering a fraction of the anger she was feeling. 'Actually, it was all Sharon's idea. And she wants you there because she considers you a friend.'

'Of the family?' Kat rose while her heart sank. Oh, no, not the Musketeers again, creating havoc with their interference. How *could* they, when they knew how she felt? Knew how she had been struggling to put her life back in order. 'That's a joke! Do you really think I'd fit in? Let me guess, service at the Cathedral and reception at the Regent——'

'Parish church and home!' he corrected her with clipped tightness. 'What is this, Kathleen, sour grapes? I thought you'd be pleased——'

'Pleased? *Pleased*!' Her nails dug into her palms, her spine rigid with pain and fury as she lost the last of her cool. 'You know what would please me? To stand up at your wedding when the minister asks if there is anyone with just cause, and shove your damned Bishop honour back down your lying throat! So maybe you'd better consider that before you walk up that aisle, Daniel! Maybe you'd better look over your shoulder. Because if *I'm* there, there won't *be* a wedding! I'll stop it in its tracks, and there won't be a damned thing that you or all your damned money and influence can do about it. I'll drag your precious name so deep in the mud that Clarissa won't touch you with a forked stick!'

Somewhere in the middle of her tirade Daniel had been jolted into action. He came around the desk with the silent speed of a black panther, and grabbed the hands that came up to strike him.

'Now, just a minute, Kathleen——'

'Get away from me, you swine! You think I can't do it? You think I won't?' Hot tears fought with her rage.

'Calm down, Kathleen——' He held her with difficulty as she struggled, kicking out at his shins.

'Calm down? Oh, yes, that's very well for you to say. You're not the one who's going to have the baby!'

He staggered back, his hand going out to the desk, knocking the phone to the floor with a crash in the horrified silence.

His secretary was at the door in a flash. 'Mr Bishop? Is everything all right?'

Daniel was staring thunderstruck at Kat, his eyes searching her face and running down over her breasts to her flat stomach. 'You're lying,' he croaked.

'Mr Bishop?' His secretary was rooted to the spot by the sight of her employer's white face. 'Are you all right?'

'What?' Daniel looked blankly at her. 'Yes, yes . . .' He waved her impatiently out and, when she didn't respond, moved over to shut the door in her face and lock it. He turned and leaned against the panels. 'You're pregnant?' he asked hoarsely.

'Yes!' Kat tilted her head with a defiance she no longer felt.

'How much?'

'Too much,' she snapped. 'I'm not getting rid of it, Daniel.'

He looked at her as if she were mad. 'I'd kill you if you did,' he said, colour pouring back into his face again, eyes so violently blue that Kat believed him. She moved nervously under the savage intensity of his stare. 'It was that first time, wasn't it? I took your virginity and gave you something equally precious in exchange. My baby.'

His almost instant possessiveness was disturbing. This wasn't the way it was supposed to go. He was supposed to be angry at the complication. This was supposed to be *her* triumph, not his!

'Aren't you going to demand proof that it's yours?' she taunted him weakly, a protective hand on her belly.

'You're here. That's all the proof I need,' he said quietly.

His trust made her feel guilty. 'And what are you going to do with that proof, Daniel?' she sneered.

'Why, marry you, of course,' he said, as though surprised that she could think there was any other alternative.

'I wouldn't marry you if you were the only man on earth!' Kat reacted furiously to his fickleness.

'As far as you're concerned, I am,' he said grimly. 'You're not going to marry any other man, Kathleen, not while I'm still breathing. What did you expect me to do? Offer you something less?'

The thought of Daniel dying made her tremble. Coming here had been a bad idea. 'You have a strange concept of honour, Daniel. I see no honour in marrying a man who's already sent out the invitations to his wedding to another woman. Does a legitimate heir mean more to you than a business deal? What a pity you can't marry *both* of us, and have the best of both worlds!'

With an explosive sound, Daniel heaved himself away from the door, and Kat flinched as he approached, but he merely walked past to scoop the offending invitation from his desk. He flicked it open and held it out to her. 'Read it.'

'I don't——'

'Read it, damn you!' He waved the serrated gold edge at her as if he would like to slit her throat with it, so she took it and scanned it contemptuously, only to freeze.

'Sharon?' The word was a thread of sound.

'And Stephen. Sharon organised it all. Even Adelaide didn't know until this morning. Sharon thought it better to present her with a *fait accompli*. She wanted to surprise everybody, she said. It seems she succeeded better than she knew.'

'I . . . I . . . I don't know what to say.'

Daniel's eyebrows rose. 'A day of firsts.' He crossed his arms over his chest and stood in an attitude of waiting as Kat tried to absorb all the implications of her misunderstanding. As she sought for an adequate explanation, Daniel reached over and took off her hat, tossing it on to his desk before recrossing his arms. 'I don't like not being able to see your face properly when you grovel,' he said, pleased with what he had revealed. 'You missed me.'

She flushed and glared at him. 'I'm not going to grovel. I . . . I made a mistake——'

'Several,' Daniel agreed, a gleam of angry satisfaction in his eyes. 'First, in assuming that I was rushing into marriage on the rebound.' She opened her mouth and he closed it with a look. 'Second, in assuming that I wouldn't want the child. And third, in barging in here instead of waiting to confront me until *after* the QueenCorp meeting.'

'What's that got to do with anything?' Kat asked sullenly.

'Because Reginald is about to announce the appointment of his daughter to the board.'

'Clarissa?' asked Kat faintly, still unable to follow his reasoning.

'The one and only. With the ultimate aim that, if she's proved herself by the time Reginald retires, she takes over the chairmanship.'

'*Clarissa?*' Kat squeaked.

'Will you listen *now?*' He was human enough to prolong her agony with a pause, to allow her to contemplate her former stupidity in denying him a hearing. 'It's what she's always wanted—a place in the business, but Reginald has some very old-fashioned ideas about women.'

'Like your father.' It was like a bright light, illuminating her brain 'And Adelaide.'

'And *her* father, yes. I could see it happening to Clarissa, the frustration of having to be content with the traditional female role when she really wanted much more. Our bargain wasn't monetary, Kat. Clarissa was happy to marry me, but she wanted my continued support and influence to persuade her father that she had a right to the same opportunities he would have given a son. She wanted, as I did, the best of both worlds. Home and family *and* a fulfilling career. Our needs seemed to mesh perfectly. Clarissa has no formal business qualifications, but you'd be surprised what she's picked up over the years of helping to entertain her father's colleagues, and she had the intelligence and the determination to have done a certain amount of study on her own. The only thing she lacks at present is confidence in her own abilities, and a certain ruthlessness when I wanted to renege on our agreement. She made it very clear I was still expected to uphold my side of the bargain as far as QueenCorp went. The secrecy was essential, Kathleen, and I owed her that much loyalty at least, after building up her hopes with other promises that I couldn't honour. I needed Reginald's goodwill while I negotiated on her behalf, and that meant maintaining the fiction of the engagement. I'm sorry, darling, for making the matter of trust such an issue when I wasn't being totally honest with you myself. But I was frustrated, and angry as hell with Clarissa for putting me in that position and with you for making me feel like a confused teenager again.

'I fully intended to marry her, you know, before you came along. We would have worked very well in harness together. I had my doubts until she confided her secret ambition, and then I thought——'

'You'd be the white knight you couldn't be for your mother.'

He smiled ruefully. 'Something like that, I suppose. I didn't realise what I would be missing until that damned triumvirate of yours sent in their walking booby-trap.' He came close, inhaled her scent and stroked a stray curl from her forehead, then traced the curve of her ear. 'I don't like your hair like this . . .it's too controlled,' he said huskily, and began to unplait it, still mesmerising her with his voice. 'After Elise, I thought I'd had my fill of passionate love, of the turmoils of youth. You exploded into my quiet skies like a comet. I wanted you so much, I didn't care how I got you, or who I walked over to do it. Once I'd bedded you, I thought that the infatuation would wane——' her hair tumbled around her shoulders and he threaded his fingers through it with a look of absorption on his beautiful face '—but it got progressively worse. I floundered around in a trap of my own making.' He was kissing her now, his words a hum against her skin, golden eyes, the point of her jaw and, at last, her mouth. His tongue was aggressive, male, deliciously familiar as it caressed her with intimate abandon. Her arms went around his neck and he drew her to him, one hand falling to the smart black buttons at the front of her dress, fumbling them undone.

'Hell, I've missed you,' he groaned, as he found her softness under the lace. 'I tried to give you time to know me, but I kept getting impatient and trying to force the pace. You wrapped yourself around my life but you wouldn't let me into yours. You wouldn't trust me enough to tell me that you wanted my love . . .' He felt her stiffen, and with a soft moan tore his mouth from its quest down her tender throat. 'It wasn't a lie, kitten. I love you. I was afraid to say it for too long, and then, when I did, I tried to make a mockery of it, in case you turned me down. Don't refuse me, Kathleen, not this time . . .'

'I . . . I don't know what you're asking,' said Kat drowningly, not really caring, only vaguely aware that he had backed her against his desk to prop her up for his kisses.

'Marry me.'

'B . . . because of the baby?'

'Because of the babies we're going to make,' he whispered against her mouth, rocking against her braced thighs, his slender fingers stroking her breast to tingling life. 'Because you're already a part of me. Didn't I tell you there might be an exception to your rule about married men? You'll sleep with me if I'm your *husband* . . .'

'You swine,' she said, totally without heat. 'You knew what I thought . . .'

'I knew . . . I was punishing you . . . and me . . . both of us, for making something which was so simple, so unutterably complicated. That night Clarissa came I really thought it was going to be all right. We had shared so much more than just our bodies, I was sure that you must sense how I felt. and yet you still *judged* me so despicably.' He shook his head. 'My brave, beautiful, confident Kathleen actually believed I could abandon her without conscience.'

'I wasn't any of those things.'

'I realised that, when it was too late. You had felt no security in my feelings because I had offered you none, just set you another of my arrogant tests to pass.'

'You said I wasn't the woman you wanted.'

'You had just flung my heart back in my face. *You* said I bored you.'

'I was hurt. It made me angry——'

'Believe me, I know *exactly* how you felt,' he said darkly. 'But my hands were tied. Reginald had got wind of some of my kite-flying at QueenCorp, and Clarissa was afraid the whole scheme was about to come tumbling down around her ears and she wouldn't have me *or* a career in the family firm. I wasn't going to come empty-handed to you again, so I decided to extricate myself from the whole mess before I made another move. You wouldn't take anything else from me, but you would damned well take my love . . .'

'That's because you were offering all the wrong things,' Kat told him. Her hands had come up under his jacket, absorbing the heat of his skin through the silk shirt.

'How could I know that? You never told me what you *did* want.'

'Because I thought you'd know why . . . that I'd loved you all along, even while *you* were only in the throes of an infatuation!'

'So you'll marry me?'

'What about your mother?' she said, striving to be sensible.

'You'll cope,' he said, with utter confidence. 'And I'll make up for any enthusiasm she lacks.' He showed her how, with mouth and hands, until they were both thoroughly aroused, his jacket and shirt unbuttoned and Kat's dress askew. A tone sounded on the desk, and Daniel cursed as his secretary's voice came through on the intercom, definitely aggrieved, reminding him of his meeting.

Daniel growled an unintelligible response and reluctantly let Kat go. The expression on his face was the same as the one he had worn that fateful night of Clarissa's visit to the penthouse, but this time Kat didn't misjudge his dilemma.

'I'm supposed to be there, too,' she said, readjusting her dress and trying to cool her cheeks with her hands. Daniel was afraid to leave anything unresolved between them, but his absence from the top table would cause untold speculation, especially in conjunction with the announcement about Clarissa. 'After all,' she teased him, 'isn't that why you sent me the shares, to try and con me along to this meeting?'

He grinned, looking almost boyish. 'Actually, there were two strings to that bow. I half hoped you would rage in to return them in person. I would play it cool and seduce you with sweet reason.'

'Mmm, you played it very cool when I walked in today,' she commented, giving up on the hat. It wouldn't look right on her love-tousled waves.

'Shock,' he confessed simply. 'I'd regretfully given up on that idea, but after today it was nothing barred.'

'What were you going to do?' she asked curiously.

'Court you with formal proof of my love.'

'Oh, Daniel!' He still didn't understand her. 'More presents?'

'Only one. A very special gift.' He went over to his desk, unlocked a drawer and took out a package, very simply wrapped in brown paper. 'Open it?'

'Now? But the meeting——'

'Can wait.'

'Arrogant as ever, Daniel,' Kat murmured as she undid the package. Inside was a box, too large for a ring. 'If this is jewellery, Daniel——'

It was. A fob watch on a chain. One she recognised instantly. His Breguet, the one he usually wore himself, his pride and joy. As elegant as its owner, it was beautifully designed and constructed, still working as well as when it was made over two hundred years ago.

'Y . . . you can't give me this,' she whispered, the timepiece warm in the cup of her hand like a living thing, the delicately worn face blurring as Kat fought a rush of tears. 'Daniel, this is the favourite piece of your entire collection.'

'It's also worth a fortune,' he said to her bent head.

'I don't care about the money.' She glared at him fiercely, and he saw the tears and something deep within him sighed in relief.

'Nor do I,' he said. He cupped her face and licked away her tears. 'It's a betrothal gift.'

'You mean you'll take it back if I don't marry you?' she said, eyes closed against his gentle assault on her face.

'No. It's yours with my love, whatever happens. I trust you to care for it the way I did. But, Kathleen, don't you know that the pleasure that the Breguet gives me is nothing to the pleasure I find in your company? Pleasure is meaningless unless it's shared.'

'Oh, Daniel, of course I'll marry you,' she cried. 'How can you think that there is even a *choice*? I meant to have you from the first moment I set eyes on you.'

To her amusement, he looked diverted and rather smug. 'Really?'

'No.' She cheerfully disillusioned him. 'I despised you. I thought you were a beautiful stuffed vegetable.'

Her words held a ring of truth that made him laugh. 'And I thought that you were a big, juicy tart.'

'You thought I was *fat*?' Kat was shocked. What was he going to think of her in a few months' time?

'Darling, calling you fat would be like calling the Venus de Milo a statue of a deformed woman,' he said drolly. 'Of course, once I got my teeth into you I knew you weren't a tart. You were . . . are . . . ambrosia. No, don't put the Breguet away, I want you to wear it. It's perfect with that dress.'

He pinned it on for her and stepped back to admire the effect.

'Everyone will know,' she said huskily. 'Clarissa——'

'Isn't wearing my ring any more, in case you didn't notice,' he replied, knowing she hadn't. 'All obligations have been hereby discharged. I want the world to know . . . and envy me.'

'You once said I'd never fit into the Bishop life-style,' she said, shaken by his supreme look of satisfaction.

'That was before I knew you.' He drew her back into his arms and said gravely, 'No more secrets, Kathleen. From now on we'll always be honest with each other, even at the expense of our pride, about what we think and feel, as well as about what we do. And we'll never knowingly hurt each other.' He buried his face in her fragrant hair, asking tentatively, 'Do you mind, about being pregnant? Am I selfish to be glad?'

She felt the loving beat of his heart against hers. 'No . . . I want it, too. I was glad, not only because it gave me a good excuse to disrupt what I thought were your cosy plans with Clarissa, but because it would always be a link with you. I love the idea of a baby.'

His hands cupped her flat stomach as another angry tone sounded from the intercom. He leaned his forehead against hers. 'Damn, if only we didn't have this meeting, we could stay locked in here all day, and I could introduce myself to my child . . .'

Kat laughed softly. 'Daniel, what would your secretary say?'

'She'd be delighted. I've been bad-tempered for weeks——'

'You? Mr Polite? Bad-tempered?' Kat batted her eyelashes at him.

'Yes, you'll have to apologise to her, because it's your fault. Even a thoroughbred can get mettlesome with a burr under its saddle.' He slapped her bottom and spun her away while he collected a sheaf of papers from his desk. 'You've put me through hell and back, Kathleen, and when this meeting is over there's going to be an accounting.'

'Mmm, sounds interesting.'

'Oh, I can promise you it'll be that. You see this desk?'

Kat blushed, and he laughed. 'I was only going to say that it's cleared of all the backlog of work that was piling up. Work was the only thing that succeeded in taking my mind off missing you. Every time I picked up a brush I wanted to paint you, and I was too impatient to work on my clocks. After the meeting we'll go upstairs and talk and make long, luscious love and let the Three Musketeers know that their ridiculous manoeuvrings have finally succeeded.' He came across and took her hand, leading her to the door which he paused to unlock.

'I'll ravish you across my desk another day, kitten,' he promised her in a wicked murmur as he opened the door.

She turned her head, eyes innocent with bewilderment. 'But, Daniel, that's not what I was thinking about. I wanted to ravish *you* on the desk . . .'

Miss Coulter blinked as the couple passed her desk. She had never seen a man more self-possessed than her employer, but she could have sworn that he was blushing. He was laughing, too, but his eyes were anything but amused. They were as hot and blue as a desert sky, and Miss Coulter felt a very sharp pang of envy in her middle-aged breast as she interpreted that look. She returned to her typing, however, content. Mr Bishop, if she wasn't mistaken, would be back to his usual silk-mannered self the next time she saw him.

She wondered when that would be . . .

Harlequin Presents®

Coming Next Month

Available in April wherever paperback books are sold, or through
Harlequin Reader Service:

In the U.S.
901 Fuhrmann Blvd.
P.O. Box 1397
Buffalo, N.Y. 14240-1397

In Canada
P.O. Box 603
Fort Erie, Ontario
L2A 5X3

This April, don't miss Harlequin's new Award of
Excellence title from

Harlequin Presents...

CAROLE MORTIMER

Award of Excellence

---

elusive as the unicorn

*When Eve Eden discovered that Adam
Gardener, successful art entrepreneur, was
searching for the legendary English artist, The
Unicorn, she nervously shied away. The Unicorn's
true identity hit too close to home....*

*Besides, Eve was rattled by Adam's
mesmerizing presence, especially in the light
of the ridiculous coincidence of their names—
and his determination to take advantage of it!
But Eve was already engaged to marry her
longtime friend, Paul.*

*Yet Eve found herself troubled by the different
choices Adam and Paul presented. If only the
answer to her dilemma didn't keep eluding her....*

HP1258-1

Harlequin Superromance®

LET THE GOOD TIMES ROLL...

Add some Cajun spice to liven up your New Year's celebrations and join Superromance for a romantic tour of the rich Acadian marshlands and the legendary Louisiana bayous.

CAJUN MELODIES, starting in January 1990, is a three-book tribute to the fun-loving people who've enriched America by introducing us to crawfish étouffé and gumbo, zydeco music and the Saturday night party, the *fais-dodo*. And learn about loving, Cajun-style, as you meet the tall, dark, handsome men who win their ladies' hearts with a beautiful, haunting melody....

Book One: *Julianne's Song*, January 1990
Book Two: *Catherine's Song*, February 1990
Book Three: *Jessica's Song*, March 1990

Harlequin Superromance

**Here are the longer, more involving stories you
have been waiting for...Superromance.**

Modern, believable novels of love, full of the complex
joys and heartaches of real people.

Intriguing conflicts based on today's constantly
changing life-styles.

Four new titles every month.
Available wherever paperbacks are sold.

SUPER-1

**NEW COMPELLING LOVE STORIES
EVERY MONTH!**

Pursuing their passionate dreams against a
backdrop of the past's most colorful and dramatic
moments, our vibrant heroines and dashing heroes
will make history come alive for you.

**HISTORY HAS NEVER BEEN
SO ROMANTIC!**

Available wherever Harlequin books are sold.